ON A RED STATION, DRIFTING

ALSO BY ALIETTE DE BODARD

OBSIDIAN AND BLOOD
Servant of the Underworld
Harbinger of the Storm
Master of the House of Darts

DOMINION OF THE FALLEN
The House of Shattered Wings
The House of Binding Thorns
The House of Sundering Flames

DRAGONS AND BLADES
Of Dragons, Feasts and Murders
Of Charms, Ghosts and Grievances

XUYA UNIVERSE
On a Red Station, Drifting
The Citadel of Weeping Pearls
The Tea Master and the Detective
Of Wars, and Memories, and Starlight
In the Shadow of the Ship (forthcoming)

XUYA UNIVERSE ROMANCES
The Red Scholar's Wake
A Fire Born of Exile

STANDALONE NOVELS
Navigational Entanglements

SHORT FICTION AND NOVELLAS
In the Vanishers' Palace
Of Books, and Earth, and Courtship

ON A RED STATION, DRIFTING

ALIETTE DE BODARD

JAB

Published by JABberwocky Literary Agency, Inc.

On a Red Station, Drifting

This paperback edition published by JABberwocky Literary
Agency, Inc. in 2024, in association with Zeno Agency LTD.
Originally published by Immersion Press in 2012 and Nine
Dragons River in 2013.

Cover art by Sinvia
Back Cover design by Tara O'Shea

ISBN 978-1-625677-34-1 (ebook)
ISBN 978-1-625677-35-8 (paperback)

JABberwocky Literary Agency, Inc.
49 W. 45th Street, Suite #5N
New York, NY 10036
http://awfulagent.com
ebooks@awfulagent.com

To the women of my family, who held everything together in the midst of the storms.

Book 1
Linh

Linh arrived on Prosper Station blown by the winds of war, amidst a ship full of refugees who huddled together, speaking tearfully of the invading armies: the war between the rebel lords and the Empire had escalated, and their war-kites had laid waste to entire planets.

Linh kept her distance, not wanting to draw attention to herself on the way there; but, when they disembarked from the mindship and joined the immigration queue, she found herself behind an old woman in a shawl, who glanced fearfully around her, as if she expected soldiers to come out of the shadows at any moment. Bent and bowed, she looked so much like Linh's long-dead mother that Linh found herself instinctively reaching out.

"It's going to be all right, Madam," she said.

The woman looked at her: past her, in that particular way of old people whose mind wasn't steady anymore. "They'll come here," she whispered, her eyes boring into Linh's, uncomfortably bright and feverish. "There is no escape."

"We're safe," Linh said.

The woman looked sceptical. Linh drew herself to her

full height, calling on a hint of the dignity and poise she'd taken when heading her tribunal sessions. "We are the children of the Emperor, and he will protect us."

The old woman looked at her for a while, as if seeing her for the first time. "If you say so, child."

"I know it to be true," Linh said. She mouthed the words, the platitudes, effortlessly, as though she believed them: a good scholar, a good magistrate, able to engage in any argument, no matter how trivial or nonsensical. Of course she knew the Emperor had no desire to engage the rebel lords; that he was young, and badly advised, and would prefer to retreat. She knew all the words. After all, her denunciation of that policy was what had tarred her with the red ink of criminals; sent her on the run to this spirits-forsaken place with nothing but her wits to rely on.

The old woman had turned away. They were almost at the beginning of the queue now, and Linh could see three men in livery, checking papers and directing refugees into the station itself. Linh took a deep breath, bracing herself. Every instinct she had called for her to slip through like the other refugees.

Every instinct but one, and she could feel, through the mem-implants, her First Ancestor Thanh Thuy's presence, the old woman as strong and querulous as ever, reminding her that ties of blood held up Heaven and Earth; that even though Linh didn't know Prosper Station and had never met the family, they were still relatives, and entitled to far more than minimal courtesies.

And, of course, as usual, First Ancestor was right.

Linh shook her head, shaking off the slight dissociation that always came with mem-implants. It was becoming harder and harder to tell implants from her own mind, a side-effect of being so good with them.

She waited until they'd checked papers, and given her the permissions that would allow her to access the trance, Prosper's internal network. Then, when the queue of refugees had wandered away in search of their fortune, she sought someone in charge, who turned out to be a young man with a quivering voice, barely old enough to have passed his exams.

"I am Lê Thi Linh," she said. Lê, like all Dai Viet names, was common. But the way she held herself, and her utter certainty, was enough to shake him.

She stood silent and unmoving as he dragged her into the trance: she got a brief flash of his credentials as Keeper of the Outer Gates for Prosper Station, and an even briefer flash of his family tree, the line of his greater ancestors lighting up in red, warm tones, all the way up until it intersected her own lineage. A cousin, somewhat removed. Hardly surprising, as most of Prosper Station came, ultimately, from the same stock that had bred her: Lê Thi Phuoc, who had borne in her womb the Honoured Ancestress and Her four human siblings.

"I see." She could see him swallow, convulsively, could track the beads of sweat on his pale skin: everything thrown into merciless clarity, as if he were a witness before her tribunal. "Welcome, Aunt Linh. I'll take you to the Inner Quarters."

She followed him, not into the refugee hall, but into another, smaller corridor and then another, until they seemed to be wandering into a maze; and, like a maze, Prosper Station unfolded its wonders to her.

In many ways, it did not belie its name. The corridors were vast and warm, decorated with hologram works of art, from images of waterfalls on the Fifth Planet, to a lonely house clinging to the mountain, lost in morning mist. Here and there, quatrains spoke of the wonders of coming home, of the sorrow of parting and the fall of the Old Empire...

In other ways...Linh had once been to the capital, and had seen the epitome of refinement there—the inlaid marble panels, brought all the way back from Old Earth, the exquisite calligraphy that breathed and seemed to move with a life of its own, like a coiled dragon hidden within text. For all its wealth, Prosper Station remained a small, isolated station at the back end of nowhere, on the edge of the Dai Viet Empire. The poems were quotations taken from old books, and not the vibrant, searing words traded in the literary clubs on First Planet; the paintings, too, were old, and looked like they hadn't been refreshed for a while; and the architecture of the corridors was a little too bulky, a little too clumsy, lacking the effortless flowing grace of more central habitats.

There was a faint music of zither in the background, which got stronger as they crossed room after room; and a faint smell, like the one after the rain. The walls flared out, and they were walking through carefully preserved gardens, with the smell of bamboo and phuong grass heavy in the air, a luxury that must have all cost a fortune in air and water and heat.

Linh felt a thread at the back of her mind: Fifth Ancestor Hoang, trying to push her into reading the poems which named each area, to admire the designers' culture, their clever allusions to the poets of the past. Fifth Ancestor, ever the poet, ever the lover of history. She pushed him back, gently, ignoring the suggestion. It wasn't time for cleverness or beauty; though Fifth Ancestor whispered in her mind that there was always time for beauty, that one who did not pause to admire beauty might as well be dead to the world.

At length, they reached a room almost hidden away amidst the greenery. The door slid open at a touch of the young man's fingers; he moved away to let Linh in.

Within, everything seemed almost bare, until she realised that the shimmer on the red walls was text. Word after word scrolled from top to bottom, almost too fast to read. Linh caught fragments about moonlight, and jade, and wild herds of trau cho soi over the plains; verse after verse, more clever allusions than her mind would ever hold, even with her mem-implants.

Beautiful.

A woman was waiting for her there, frozen in the uncertain land between youth and old age, too old to be patronised, too young to be respected. Behind her was a younger girl, waiting with her head bowed, though everything in her spoke of arrested flight. "Be welcome here, cousin." A brief burst of trance, and Linh was tracing the trees. Yes, they were indeed cousins, through her maternal grandmother, and the woman's marriage to Lê Nhu Anh, and...

The world wobbled and crumpled, as if it were a sheet of paper the spirits had punched through. There was a presence in the room; the text shimmered, the letters becoming subtly distorted, the red of the walls taking on an oily sheen, like fish sauce mixed with grease, and a wind too cold to be any draught. It was all she could do not to fall to her knees, her mind struggling to cope with it all...

She hadn't come unprepared, of course. She'd read all about the stations, all about the Minds that held and regulated them, all about stations like Prosper and its Honoured Ancestress, and the family that peopled its core. But the truth of a Mind's presence shattered the easy descriptions, the facile, clever similes written as glibly as inferior poems: it was its own self, the vast, dark presence that seemed to fold the air around itself, wrapped around the contraption in the centre of the room that might have been a throne, that might have been a tree with too many thorns; metal, twisting and buckling like a fish caught on land, its shifting reflections hurting her eyes...

"Welcome home, child," a voice said, filling her ears to bursting.

"Great-great-grandmother." She forced herself to get the words out, even as the trance went wild, seeking a pathway that would connect her to the Mind, ancestor after ancestor overlaid over the twisting texts. "I apologise for disturbing you."

A sound which might have been laughter. "Nonsense. Whenever did my children ever disturb me? This is your house, and you're always welcome here."

Even the words were wrong, subtly off, evoking a burst of recognition from First Ancestor Thanh Thuy, vocabulary and phrases reminding Linh of old memorials, not used for many generations. She triggered her mem-implants, letting First Ancestor's mem-fragments flood her mind, picking out words as they surfaced. "Heaven and Earth have overturned for me. I seek refuge in the embrace of my family."

Another vast, ineffable sound: a chuckle or a sniff of anger? The pressure against her mind didn't seem unfriendly. "This was your great-grandfather's home. It's also yours, should you wish it. What is it that you seek refuge from?"

Linh hesitated a fraction of a second, as all six ancestors in her mind howled at her for daring to lie to a superior; and then said, each word as dry as sun-baked chillies on her tongue, "War has come to the Twenty-Third Planet, and to the province of Great Light. My tribunal burns in the riots, and lawless soldiers scour the streets with their war-kites, raping and pillaging as they go."

It was untrue. The news of the war had reached her only after her ship pulled itself out of the deep planes: pictures of her tribunal in flames, the litany of the dead, of the missing she couldn't trace. All because her first lieutenant Giap had tricked her into running, into abandoning her own people...

For a moment, a bare, agonising moment, a suspended breath, she thought the Mind had caught her. She felt her pulse race in its wide-spectrum vision, caught the sheen of sweat on her brow, or ten thousand other ways she could have given herself away. But at length, the pressure retreated; and in the centre of the room, the core was inert again, and the only memory of the Mind's presence in the room was a faint whisper: "You have my blessing, child."

Linh bowed, very low, as low as she'd have bowed for the Emperor, letting a dozen heartbeats pass before she rose again.

The woman, Lê Thi Quyen, was waiting for her, as unmoving and as expressionless as propriety required. "Come, Cousin," she said. "We'll see you settled properly." But as she turned away from the core Linh caught the slight, impatient shake of her head, and knew the Mind might have believed her, but Quyen would be watching, and waiting, on the lookout to expose her lies.

She might be family, as the Mind had said. But she wasn't welcome on Prosper Station.

Quyen hadn't expected Cousin Linh.

Not her coming, of course; that particular surprise couldn't have been avoided, though Quyen had known of Linh's presence only a few instants after Linh had approached the Keeper of the Outer Gate. The man had sent out a message about a relative seeking refuge; the message had been relayed through the network by means of the trance, picked up by the Honoured Ancestress Herself, and by Quyen a few heartbeats later.

But Quyen had believed Linh would be a young, bedraggled woman, bowing her head and humbly begging her distant relatives for shelter.

None of that had turned out to be true. Cousin Linh had bowed, to be sure, but it was with the stiff grace of people unused to obeisance. Even bowed, she'd held herself with quiet, easy arrogance, and spoken with the lilted, old-fashioned speech characteristic of scholars. Her gaze had wandered from time to time, each time for a fraction of a second, enough for Quyen to guess Linh was communicating with several mem-implants; that her speech, her manners would have been coached by ghost images of her own ancestors, honed to perfection like the design of a mindship.

In short, Linh was everything Quyen wasn't: a success at the exams, the greater partner in a marriage, should she so choose. Linh would never be sent away to broker a trade alliance, would never have to produce children to be judged worthy, and her work was admired and praised within the Dai Viet Empire. Unlike Quyen, who was little better than a brood-mare.

And a failure even at that. Quyen had no children; and her husband, like so many greater marriage partners, had been called away by the necessities of the war. He'd left one bright morning on a mindship, and he'd been gone for so long without news that Quyen found herself forgetting even the sound of his voice.

"You look thoughtful," the Honoured Ancestress said. The familiar, reassuring pressure slid against her mind, a reminder that she might not have mem-implants, but that she wasn't alone.

"Just wondering what to do with Cousin Linh," Quyen lied. She felt ashamed of where her thoughts dragged her, but the woman rubbed her the wrong way—something in the tilt of her head, in her casual arrogance, in her behaviour, typical of someone who'd always had the world go their way and couldn't even have the grace to bow when it abased her.

The Honoured Ancestress's pressure ebbed and flowed, as it often did when She was considering a problem. "We are not short of postings on Prosper Station," She said.

"No," Quyen said. She thought of where Linh might go. The overcrowded and underfunded tribunal? She would find it an insult to be the lackey of an existing magistrate, especially so soon after losing her own responsibilities. And did Quyen really want her in the velvet cap and jade robes, lording it over them all? As a supplicant, she was arrogant enough; as a representative of the Dragon Throne...

"The girls' tutor has resigned," she said, aloud. She called up the distribution of allowances all over the station. A tutor's allowance was well below the ordinary salary of a magistrate, but she could increase it enough that it wouldn't show too much. Cousin Linh would smart, but she'd recover.

"You think..." the Honoured Ancestress said.

"Of course," Quyen said, smoothly, hardly believing that her voice wasn't shaking. "Who better than a state official to prepare the girls for their examinations?"

The Honoured Ancestress said nothing. She didn't need to. Tutor, even to a ruling family, was reserved for those who hadn't gone beyond the Provincial or Planetary examination. For someone like Linh, who had passed the Metropolitan exam, and received her posting from the hands of the Emperor himself...

"Beggars don't choose what is given to them," Quyen said, aloud.

"You know best," the Honoured Ancestress said, at last. She left most human affairs to Quyen, judging Herself incapable of understanding the human heart and mind. She kept the station's systems running, from the trance to the holo-displays, from helping mindships dock to picking music and poetry for the various areas, from providing supplies and food that suited everyone, to supporting the virtual environments that would please the eyes and the ears. But still She believed that She didn't understand them.

"Of course I don't," Quyen said; and it was the unadorned, bald truth. But she knew the Honoured Ancestress would not believe her.

"You do, child. You should trust in yourself more," the Honoured Ancestress said, and Her voice was sad. The pressure against Quyen's mind withdrew; the Honoured Ancestress had left, finding something else aboard Prosper that required Her full attention.

Quyen turned to the other matters for the day: the supplies she owed for the war effort, which had to be put aboard a merchant ship and sent back to the First Planet, their own dwindling stock of food. She studied the Honoured Ancestress's star-views to determine which ships were on their way to them. There would be a strong influx of merchant ships soon, an ideal time to replenish their supplies—provided, of course, they had actually had what Prosper needed. The war had depleted everyone's resources, and merchants were liable to be boarded by any of the two rebel armies, the contents of their holds used to support the space sectors in open rebellion.

Quyen was down to reviewing the order of the day for the Assignment of Resources meeting, when a blink in the corner of her field of view indicated a priority message. She slipped into the trance to view it.

It was from Xuan Rua, the eldest of her nieces, uncharacteristically brief and to the point: "Come to Eastern Gate. Now." If it had been paper the ink would have bled, and the letters hung slightly askew. But it was simulated calligraphy, always neat and perfect no matter what happened, and the only indication of the high emotion behind it was the curt, unornamented style.

Eastern Gate. One of the entrances to the family's Inner Quarters, not the grandest, or the most accessible. What could possibly—

She was wasting time. Xuan Rua wouldn't have summoned her for anything less than an emergency. Quyen put away the papers she was using. She wondered, for a brief moment, if she should call up the surveillance sensors' feed in the trance. But she couldn't do that and move, and it would only waste time.

Instead, she ran. It was slightly undignified, considering her position as Administrator of Prosper Station, but propriety be damned. Eastern Gate. She crossed courtyards with vegetation, both the stunted low-oxygen varieties, and the more expensive ones imported from planetside; and practically shoved citizens out of the way as she ran.

She rushed through the silent library, where she saw one of her younger sisters-in-law give her a startled look from her seat; and then Quyen left her behind: going onwards, past corridor after corridor with the words of poets and statesmen blinking on the walls, the colours shifting from red to green as she ran.

Eastern Gate was small, barely a hole in a wall, surrounded by a few plants to make it appear grander than it really was. Quyen heard the argument long before she reached Eastern Gate: the Honoured Ancestress was doing Her best to muffle the voices, but Her systems had limits, and She couldn't completely change the walls' texture. They had been conceived to reflect sound as much as possible, to ensure that anyone who entered the Inner Quarters would pass from the noise of the world into a quieter environment.

Three people stood before the closed gate, darker shapes against the vivid red of the welcome signs: Xuan Rua, her uncle Bao, and...

She should have known. The third person standing there—though standing was an overstatement, since he clung to the panels of the gates, probably the only things that prevented him from collapsing like a punctured habitat—was Brother Huu Hieu, Xuan Rua's father.

"Drunk again?" she asked, coldly, to Xuan Rua, who was hovering, uncertain whether to come closer or not. "Or gambling again?" From Xuan Rua's grimace, she knew it was both.

Still, it was hardly an emergency, save that the scandal had never been this spectacular.

"Sister." Huu Hieu's speech was slurred, the accents on the words almost mangling everything past recognition. "Fancy seeing you there."

Quyen made her voice as cold and sobering as the void of space. "Your wife would be ashamed to see you." Quyen's sister-in-law had left three years ago, along with nearly all of the family's greater spouses, called to other planets by the war. Many ships from the war-zones had docked since, but none of them had brought her back. Or any of them back.

Huu Hieu laughed, attempting to pull himself upwards, failing and ending cross-legged on the floor, pathetic. "My wife? She's not coming back, Sister, and that's the truth of it. They're not coming back, any of them. The war has gobbled them up."

"Nonsense."

"Nonsense? The Russian czars did it, you know: pick up people from where they lived, and strand them back at the other end of the country after their service was done.

If the state ever came for you, you ran and hid. That's what we should have done. Run and hide."

Ever the coward, the unsubtle, unaware of propriety or decorum. Sometimes, she wondered what her sister-in-law saw in the man. Theirs had been a marriage of convenience, but they had genuinely cared for one another, much like Quyen had come to care for her own husband.

"They did their duty to Dai Viet, and to the Son of Heaven, which is more than can be said of you. Get inside," Quyen said. "Sober up, and we'll talk in the morning."

From the corner of her eye she saw Xuan Rua throw glances at her uncle Bao. Bao hadn't moved, remaining standing in the corridor, as if everything passed him right by. And perhaps it did. Bao had been retreating further and further from the world ever since his own wife had been called to service.

"Uncle, please."

Bao hesitated, and then nodded. "My eldest niece won't say it because he's her father and deserves her respect, but I have no such boundaries. We think that he's traded away his mem-implants."

That stopped her. She'd been bending over Huu Hieu, trying to coax him to stand, and now she looked at him anew. His hair hung askew, freed from the topknot of officials' spouses, his eyes bleary, the veins splayed on his cornea like a spatter of blood on a pristine floor. Her hands, searching, combed the matted hair, far heavier than it should have been, now that she thought of it. For a long, long while, nothing made a noise, as if the entire station were holding its breath; her fingers parting strand after strand, readying a silent apology to her ancestors for touching her brother-in-law, if she should be proved wrong…

There.

Her hands found the shaved patches of the skull where the mem-implants had been affixed, traced their outlines. Instead of old bone growth she found a slight yield, like the broken shell of a crab, and her hands came back with the strong, acrid smell of disinfectant.

"You're right," she said without looking at Bao or Xuan Rua. "Someone's cut into his skull." And, if they'd gone to that much trouble to keep it hidden, they wouldn't have just taken a look, either.

His mem-implants. All that was left of his ancestors, to advise him through life. A favour he didn't deserve. He was no official and should have been as devoid of implants as Quyen; but his family had had no other descendants, and thus no one else to take care of the ancestral altars. How could he possibly think of selling those?

"Who took them?" she asked. If you weren't kin to the persona stored in a mem-implant, the affixing procedure had a strong chance of driving you insane; but there were always those hankering for the knowledge they brought: students desperate to pass the imperial examinations and attain the status of a state official.

"Who cares?" Huu Hieu's speech was slurred again, his eyes rolling up in their orbits. She'd thought it was an excess of drink; but it might have been the side-effects of the anaesthesia. "As if you ever did, sister. Frigid bitch…"

"You're making a fool of yourself, elder brother," Bao snapped, and something in his voice must have reached Huu Hieu, because he mumbled something indistinct before his eyes closed, and didn't open again.

"I don't think he's in a state to tell us," Xuan Rua said, cautiously.

Quyen sat, cradling Huu Hieu in her lap, breathing in the sickening smell of alcohol mingled with the gods knew what. Sold them. Given them away. She didn't care if he sold or dishonoured his own ancestors—that was his own problem, and he was welcome to it! But one of the mem-implants he'd so casually disposed of wasn't his but his wife's.

They had, as was customary, traded implants so that they could access the higher functions of the station, and have direct contact with the Honoured Ancestors, both on Prosper and on Huu Hieu's natal station.

One of Huu Hieu's implants belonged to them. To Prosper. To the Honoured Ancestress. One of the family's treasures that Quyen had been responsible for, as she was responsible for the rest of the station. What would the Honoured Ancestress think? She shirked from the picture, as fractured and as cold as a blade of ice driven through her ribs.

"What do you know?" she asked.

"Not much, sorry," Bao said. "I picked him up rimwards, in one of the gambling circles."

"And you thought something was off? Why the mem-implants specifically?"

"I…I can't tell you." Bao's hand made a sign, tracing

17

Xuyan characters for "Peach Garden". It was a reminder of a brotherhood oath, which would weigh as heavily as family ties.

"I see," Quyen said, slowly. "Have you any idea who took them?"

Bao shook his head. "The Tile and Deer Abode. That's all I have."

"I see." Quyen let go of Huu Hien, letting him fall to the ground far more softly than she'd have wished to. "I need to think about the best way to handle this." And to Xuan Rua: "Can you take him home?"

Her niece appeared on the verge of tears, but she nodded. Quyen said, as gently as she could, "Master Kong himself said that a man's duty to a superior included steering them away from evil acts. You did no wrong."

Xuan Rua swallowed audibly, and came to lift her father's prone body. "I'll see you tomorrow," Quyen said, rising.

Back in her quarters she straightened the holos of her own ancestors: her parents-in-law, and her own parents, who had given her in marriage to Prosper Station as part of a trade alliance. She disrobed, slowly, looking into their eyes. She had no mem-implants to remember them. Those had gone to her elder sister, who had passed the imperial examinations and become a state official, while Quyen herself remained the lesser partner of a marriage, managing the daily business of her house, and waiting for her husband Anh to come back.

To come back; to give her a son and to confirm the

status she had on Prosper; to look at her with wonder in his eyes, and see how worthy of him she'd become...

She said, aloud, "You didn't call me."

There was the familiar feeling of the world twisting around her, and the touch on her mind, strong enough to hold her against all storms. "I didn't hear anything until my grandniece sent her message." The Honoured Ancestress's voice was fainter than usual, as if coming from a great distance.

"But you heard," Quyen said.

"From the moment my attention was called to Eastern Gate, yes, I heard it all. The implant that was lost... it holds the memory of Du Khach. She's old, from the generation of your grandparents, but I remember her as though it were yesterday. She'd roam through the outer circles, peeking behind panels and trying to understand how the Station worked, and sit with me late in the evenings, listening to my ramblings. I can see her, shaping environments within the heart-room, so we could sit together and have tea..." The pressure against Quyen's mind became warm, tinged with a bitter sweetness. "No wonder she made herself into a designer of mind-ships and space stations in the end. She made us all proud."

Quyen said nothing. She had not known Du Khach; and could barely even imagine what the passage of time would mean for the Honoured Ancestress. To see them all, from birth to senility and death, and yet go on, taking the children under Her wing, even while knowing they, too, would die...

19

"Child?" the Honoured Ancestress said. The trance-link was tinged with sadness, like unshed tears. "Will you find it, daughter? It...it means much to me."

Daughter. The emphasis was unmistakable. Quyen thought of herself a decade ago: a frightened young girl just off the ship, praying that her husband would be kind; and of the strange sheen rising around her, the all-encompassing embrace that took her in, and asked nothing back. Nothing, save her love and piety; and were they not such a small price to pay?

"Of course I'll find them," Quyen said. She could taste salt on her tongue, and an acrid bitterness. "I won't disappoint you. But promise me you won't strain yourself too much. You can't care for us all."

"I'm not mortal, child."

She wasn't human. She might have been borne in a human womb, She might share an ancestress with Quyen's husband, but She'd been designed from optics and fibres and nanobots and She'd lived far beyond human lifetimes. But She was...

Quyen dared not voice the thought; and one did not contradict an elder. "You have limits."

The Honoured Ancestress made a sound that sent chills up Quyen's arms, which might have been laughter, which might have been tears. "We all do. Good night, child." And with that, she was gone, leaving Quyen in the silence of the empty room.

Linh was bored. Giving lessons to two young girls, no

matter how gifted or dedicated, was a task for menials, and certainly did not require a holder of an exalted Metropolitan degree, much less a former magistrate.

She did everything Quyen had asked of her—provided essay topics, and hammered the classics into their heads until they breathed the words of the ancients with every step.

Today, after the usual drills, she dragged them into the trance where she had them superimpose an environment of their own design onto reality, without asking the Honoured Ancestress for help. It was an exercise requiring one to walk on the knife's edge between focus and flow, at which Linh herself had excelled, but had seldom practised since her student days.

And they were both failing miserably at it.

They were meant to work together, and had picked a deliberately old-fashioned environment: the interior of an Exodus spaceship from Old Earth, gleaming with obsolete boards and control panels, and obscure parts the purpose of which had long vanished in history. The basic structure was sound, but here and there, the illusion flickered as if it were falling apart, and cracks had appeared everywhere in the metal walls, spreading further and further the more Linh watched.

The youngest and most ambitious of the sisters, Xuan Kiem, seemed unusually distracted, though she did her best to hide it. Her sister Xuan Rua, who usually assisted Quyen in the day-to-day running of Prosper, was worse; barely listening to anything Linh had to say.

"Enough," Linh said, waving a hand. "That will be all for today."

The illusion flickered and died, and the girls emerged from the trance, blinking furiously. Xuan Kiem looked as though she might approach Linh, but Xuan Rua made a gesture towards her and the two of them scattered, fleeing the courtyard like startled sparrows.

What was going on? It was frustrating—no, infuriating—to be cut out of any responsibilities. But not being informed of important matters was worse. More than ever, it made Linh feel an exile, and wonder whether she had made the right decision in coming to Prosper.

She missed Giap, more than ever. Her tribunal's first lieutenant would found the words to comfort her, to remind her of her purpose. Her ancestors on the mem-implants could do that. But their advice was hollow, dispensed by poor copies of men and women long settled into the afterlife.

Giap...

Giap was back on the Twenty-Third Planet, and likely he had died in the invasion. The thought weighed in her stomach like a cold stone. She was alone now, swimming upstream in an unknown, dangerous country, not knowing anything of what lay on the banks, or where the river took its source.

She felt First Ancestor Thanh Thuy's amusement. *The fish who finds the source becomes a dragon.*

Yes, there was that. She had leapt the falls of the examinations, risen up as an official, and made her own way in the world. She was no harmless frog; she was a dragon, and her place wasn't here in this dingy school, teaching girls who had no need of her services to succeed at the examinations. Xuan Kiem would pass by virtue of her talents, and the eldest, Xuan Rua, obviously had no interest in anything but Prosper.

Like Cousin Quyen.

Her hands itched. She was tired of being idle, of being blinded and kept in the dark.

Fine.

If Cousin Quyen wanted her servile, Linh wasn't going to oblige her. Ever since she'd arrived, the family had kept her busy, either under Quyen's orders, or those of the Honoured Ancestress. When her lessons with the girls were finished, a woman would come and ask her opinion of a poem; or the girls' uncle, Bao, would casually stroll in, and discuss Buddhist texts with her. It could have been coincidence, but there had been too many such events. For whatever reason, Cousin Quyen wanted Linh busy, and not wandering around the station.

Which was precisely what Linh was going to do.

She walked out of her quarters, and into the wide courtyard of the common area. No one stopped her. She guessed she had a little time before the girls went to Quyen. And perhaps more, if the family was affected by whatever had distracted them.

She headed out, towards the outer rings, passing under the wide gates of the family quarters. As she moved away from the core of the station the crowd changed. The red-clad workers in livery were replaced by grey-clad techs and movers of bots. Then the crowd itself seemed to mould, taking on the vivid colours of the hundreds of people on the station: the poets, the scholars, the Masters of Wind and Water, the Commissioners of Supplies, and the myriad of people who made life aboard the station possible.

Linh let herself be carried away by the flow, past large complexes tucked away behind grey facades, and shops selling everything from medicine to scrolls and holo-displays. But, as she did so, her magistrate's mind was still working, and her enhanced vision was making notes of all the small details: how the store fronts were almost empty; how people with gaunt faces loitered in the streets, hesitating over whether to accost someone; how the crowd that watched the xanh-insects fight kept glancing sideways, their eyes not on the fight, but on other, more serious matters.

It was obvious that the station was falling inwards, taking in more refugees than it could afford to, or perhaps redistributing food in an inefficient manner. Not surprising, given Quyen's inexperience. She did a creditable job, but when it came down to it, she was the lesser partner in a marriage, and had not been trained to handle anything as large as Prosper Station.

Not that Linh had been, of course. But at least she could help. At least she could offer something valuable in exchange for the risks Quyen was taking in sheltering her, something more than anyone with a smidgeon education could have done.

At last, she found herself in front of a simple grey

façade, with rows of elegant characters flashing yellow on a white background, both in Xuyan and in the Viet language. They read: Hall of Network Access.

She paused. She'd thought she was following nothing but her inclination, taking crossroads at random, following the sounds and smells that appealed to her most. But she was magistrate, with the mem-implants of six ancestors in her mind. One of those, Fourth Ancestor Canh, had lived on the station a hundred years ago, and he would know the layout. Had she accessed her mem-implants without realising, letting half-remembered knowledge guide her here?

Did she want so badly to know what had happened, back on the Twenty-Third Planet?

Of course she did. Of course she owed Giap and her other lieutenants; Ho and her poetry club, and the hundred people she had run away from like a coward.

She should have stayed. Demons strike her! She should have stayed.

Without being aware that she did so, she pulled the bead curtain apart, and entered a dark room, lit only by flame-lamps. The man sitting behind the counter looked oddly familiar, the way everyone on the station did, with their lines distorted by generations of interbreeding. He nodded at her, pointing towards a free terminal.

Linh sat and composed herself in the silence. The terminal was a single holo-projector, offering her a map of options arranged in the shape of a planet system—a fitting touch on a space station.

As usual, the atmosphere was quiet, everyone immersed in their own private worlds. Linh slipped on her headphones. She suspected she didn't need them, and that the station's Mind would be ensuring the sound from her unit remained contained around her, within the four low walls that made up her cubicle. But still, it never hurt to be prudent.

There was a message, sent as private mail to her personal account. It came from someone styled "Humble Servant of the Green Wood". Puzzled, Linh opened it. And saw Giap.

Her heart stopped; then did an odd lurch within her chest, draining her of blood. She could do nothing but stare at him. He was pale and dishevelled. His hair, which he'd always worn in a top-knot, was hacked quite short, and he looked as though he'd aged ten years in days— his skin wrinkled, his hair white, giving him the air of a truly old man, rather than the youthful, fatherly figure she remembered.

"Magistrate. I trust you are doing well. By now, you will have learnt of what befell the planet." He looked away from the recording device with a grimace. "Your tribunal is in shambles. I apologise, but all that we could save were a handful of people. There were many deaths. Civilians mainly, caught in the first attack, when the war-kites swooped down and bombarded the district."

His gaze was distant, his fists clenched. Linh ached to be able to speak to him, to support him with her stern, unmoving face, reassuring him that he was doing the right thing, just as he had reassured her when her faith in the Empire's justice system faltered.

But he wasn't there, couldn't see her; and even the message was days old now, carried through on one of the ships that had recently docked at Prosper.

"The forces of Lord Soi hold the cities," Giap said. "I have taken the liberty of taking citizens with me into the wilderness, away from their influence. You were right, magistrate." Giap's face did not waver. "We have faith this will be proved."

He meant he was fighting them with whatever means he could: militia, guerrilla. He was waiting for reinforcement from the Empire, for the Emperor to send soldiers to reclaim the conquered provinces.

It would never happen. The thought was a fist of ice, tightening around her heart. This was what she'd railed against in her memorial to the Dragon Throne, the same one that had sent her into exile: the cowardice of the ministers, who kept urging the Emperor to safeguard the heart of the nation, to retreat from the armies of the rebel lords, again and again, evacuating his own people ahead of the enemy.

She had urged the Emperor to call up armies, to unite the Empire once again under his rule...

She had known, even then, that the memorial would not be heeded. She had written it because it was her moral duty, as First Ancestor Thanh Thuy had pointed out; and because, if Heaven smiled down on her, it would be part of a flood of similar memorials from other scholars;

enough to have the Emperor reconsider his position. But the chances of that happening? Minuscule, as insignificant as a single man to a star or a black hole.

Giap should have known that, too. He should have. He was smarter than this, more world-wise and cynical than this. He couldn't pin his hopes on a rescue that wouldn't come. Linh cut the message, and switched on her own camera to record a reply.

"Listen," she said. "There is no help coming, Giap. You have to come back into the city. Trickle back, pretend you fled the invasion and are now returning home." As she had, too. And what did that make her? "Lord Soi won't harm civilians. He wouldn't dare, or the entire province would rise against him. You have to stop this foolishness. The Empire has forsaken you. There is no help coming. Do you understand me? This is an order."

An order from a magistrate who had run away, who had let Giap talk her into abandoning her own people. He'd talked about hiding until it all blew over, that the Emperor would soon forget her if he couldn't arrest her. And she'd listened. Ancestors take him! She'd let him push her into a ship, and into another and before she knew it war had come, and she was on the other end of the galaxy with no ship to bring her back, powerless to do anything but watch.

She'd run away. She was father-and-mother of her people, and she'd run away like a coward, leaving them in this extremity. Leaving Giap in danger. "You have to stop," she whispered, and had to fight to prevent her voice from breaking. "Or they'll kill you."

She ended the message then, wondered if she should leave the last few moments of it intact. Giap wouldn't appreciate her breaking down, would take her to task for showing more than detached concern for underlings.

But, she thought savagely, it was all true, and she couldn't change it. Couldn't do anything but pray to the Buddha and her ancestors—the dead ones, not the simulacrums in the mem-implants—that her message would arrive, that he would listen to it.

Demons take her! She should never have left her province, never have come to Prosper. Now she was stuck, and it would cost her a fortune she didn't have to leave.

Annoyed in spite of herself, she rose and made for the exit. The man at the counter nodded at her. He'd already taken the amount of the connection from her account, though she felt no desire to drop into the trance and check that he hadn't overcharged her.

"Cousin?" a voice asked.

Linh looked up, not entirely sure who to expect. The voice was male and couldn't be Quyen.

It was Cousin Huu Hieu, the father of her pupils, whom she saw but distantly when he came in to see his daughters study. He looked as clean-cut as usual, though the aura of desperation that always surrounded him hadn't gone away. It looked worse, if anything, and tinged with the stale smell of guilt. If she'd been in her tribunal, she'd have arrested him.

But she wasn't in her tribunal anymore. She was merely Cousin Linh, a menial teacher, a stranger even though she was among family. "I didn't know you sought wisdom from abroad," she said, half-mocking. A twisted quotation, the beginnings of a literary game she'd played countless times during her studies.

Huu Hieu looked up at her, as if he'd been starving and she'd handed him a loaf of bread. "We study the past so that we may know the future. Why not study abroad, so that we may know ourselves?"

Linh smiled. "It has been said that foreigners who do not follow the way of the Former Emperors will sway the masses; that they should be courteously welcomed, given one interview, one banquet…"

"… and escorted back under guard to where they came from." Huu Hieu's voice was quiet, almost wondering. Behind him, the environment deepened. She felt him drag her into the trance, and opened herself up.

Like his daughters a few hours ago, he'd used the network to design an environment. Unlike them, he was in supreme control. A country of rolling hills, impossibly wide, opened up under the brilliant blue of the Heavens: a colour Linh hadn't seen in so many months that it was almost blinding. There was the gurgle of a river, the soft noise of geese flying overhead, and a faint sound in the background, whispered over and over, that Linh finally identified as a poem. It was a lament for separated friends, watching the moon rise over different planets.

"It's beautiful," Linh whispered.

Huu Hieu hadn't moved. He now wore the long, flowing robes of a scholar. They kept shimmering in and out of focus, a deliberate effect. He didn't seem to believe in his worth as a scholar. "It's nothing. Nothing that you wouldn't be able to do twice over, if you knew Prosper's systems."

"No," Linh said, knowing that, even if she got used to Prosper's trance, even if she understood enough of the Honoured Ancestress's inner workings, she would never be able to manipulate the environment that finely. She knew she would never be able to match the sheer fragile beauty of this, like a budding rose before the frost.

"I know only small things," she said. "Tricks to impress the common folks. Nothing like this."

Huu Hieu shook his head, clearly unconvinced. Behind him, the sun was sinking below the horizon, bathing the hills in reddish lights. The geese were still there, a faint cry like the memory of sorrow.

Linh hunted for another subject of conversation, and settled on the obvious. "I was surprised to see you in the Hall of Network Access. I didn't think anyone in the family was interested in what lay outside the station."

Huu Hieu's hands clenched and his clothes reverted to the ones he wore in real-time. "For many people, Prosper is all there is under the Heavens."

She gave him the obvious answer as the moon rose, bathing the scene in a soft white light, and the stars lit up in the sky like a myriad hairpin wounds. "But not for you?"

"I…I wasn't born here." He looked uneasy and didn't elaborate.

"You're trapped here," Linh said, a feeling she knew all too well.

"Trapped, yes. I…My wife will come home soon, that's what they all say. I just have to wait and she'll be back. We'll be a family again." He laughed, bitterly. "For some, it's the only bearable thought."

She wondered for whom. Clearly not for him. He had the air of a caged bird, one who had just discovered that the bars were of steel, and that the door would only open on the day of the slaughter.

Huu Hieu said, "I read the news, you know. More and more planets are falling. They're winning."

"The rebels?" Linh shrugged. "They're badly over-stretched." They'd hold the planets they'd conquered, but soon wouldn't attack any more, not if they wanted to keep what they had. On the other hand…how bold would they get, if they knew the Emperor wasn't coming to get back what was lawfully his?

"The warring lords. You've read the histories. The Trinh and Nguyen ravaging Dai Viet, tearing it apart."

"While the puppet Emperor watched, powerless?" She raised an eyebrow. "We're stronger than that, I should think."

But still not strong enough to hold the Twenty-Third Planet. Still not strong enough to be with her people, to be by Giap's side, and advise him before he threw away his life.

Around them, the hills were…not quite right. Linh watched the grass rippling in moonlight for a while, and saw that though the blades bent in the wind, there were patches of blackness: holes and cracks in the simulation, too small to come from Huu Hieu. If he'd lost control, it would have been more spectacular than this. "Something is wrong," she said.

"I know." Huu Hieu grimaced. "They've been showing up everywhere in designed environments lately. I think the Honoured Ancestress is stretched to breaking point with so many people on the station. Maintaining personal settings for so many people is getting to Her."

Linh knew nothing of how Minds worked, either on ships or on stations. And it made little sense. Most refugees didn't get privileges that would allow them to design environments. She had them, but only because she was family and it was necessary for her work, her menial drudge dreamed up by Quyen. "If you say so," she said.

"If it bothers you..." Huu Hieu shrugged, and waved his hands. The simulation fell away to be replaced by the space in front of the Hall of Network Access. "Better? Let's walk home."

Linh merely followed him through the corridors. They were all but deserted now. The people gone back to their shifts, and the shop-fronts were closed. It looked like a different world.

Huu Hieu said, at last, his face set, "I'm not a fool. I've seen the news. I've read what they won't tell us. What the Honoured Ancestress knows, what Quyen knows. My wife's ship went into a war zone to oversee the evacuation of a planet, and never came back."

"That doesn't mean..." Linh started, but he cut her off.

"Of course it does. Spirits, we can be such children sometimes." He rubbed the back of his head thoughtfully, his hands tracing the contour of something she couldn't place. "She's dead, and there's nothing to hold me here."

"Your children."

"My children are adults." He laughed again, a queer sound, without amusement. "Ancestors, one of them is even helping Quyen run Prosper Station."

"You can't abandon them..." She paused then. Fourth Ancestor Canh was in her mind, reminding her that it was children who had duties to their parents, and not the reverse. "I apologise. It's not for me to tell you what to do."

He bowed a fraction, younger to elder, though by family standards she was younger than him, the child from a younger branch. "One should always dispense advice and wisdom."

It might have been sincere and unsubtle, but it was, in fact, deeply ironic. Quyen had been wrong to call him a blundering fool. "One should always follow one's own advice," Linh said, with a quick quirk of her lips.

She saw him smile at that and, for a bare moment, he was like a carefree child, much younger than even the youngest of his children. But then his face darkened again, looking at the red characters which marked the entrance of the inner circle.

Trapped. She wondered how she'd feel if she knew that Prosper Station was the entire bounds of her universe, that no ship would come to bear her away, that she had no place to return to...

"If you're ever..." She shook her head, unsure of how to phrase the sentence. "I might not design environments as beautiful as yours, but I do have books. Poetry and annals, and vids of historical events. If you ever want to discuss them…"

First Ancestor Thanh Thuy tried to object that it was hardly proper, that Linh would have been the greater partner in a marriage. He would remain the lesser one as long as his wife's body weren't found. Their meeting alone was as good as adultery.

She knew that, all of it. But it was a risk she was willing to bear for the sake of a little compassion.

Huu Hieu went white, as if she'd slapped him. Linh was mentally composing a suitable apology when he spoke again: "That's…very kind of you. I'll keep it in mind."

And with that he walked away, fast, not looking at her, his whole body rigid with an emotion she couldn't name.

"You shouldn't, you know," a voice said.

Linh almost jumped to the ceiling. She looked up to see Cousin Bao, Huu Hieu's absent-minded brother-in-law.

"How did you know we were here?" she asked, not bothering to signal respect.

Cousin Bao shrugged. "The Honoured Ancestress knows, doesn't she. She tracks everyone on Prosper, and lets Quyen know about significant events. It's for their own good," Bao said.

For their own good. Like Quyen set tasks for Linh's own good. "And you live with this?" she said.

Bao shrugged. But of course he knew no other law. He'd been raised on another station, and could envision no existence that wasn't shackled to a Mind.

Aliette de Bodard

"You might follow Quyen's orders," Linh said, defiantly. "But I do what I want."

Bao said nothing for a while. At length, his face carefully neutral, he said, "Allow your elder cousin to offer you some advice, for what it's worth. Prosper Station is… different."

Meaning there were rules, and she wasn't the one enforcing them; no longer a magistrate in her tribunal. Meaning they could do anything to her: give her a job that was an insult, track her even in her free time, dictate who she could see and not see.

"Different," Linh said, struggling to keep her voice even. "Hell brought into the Heavens."

"Nothing keeps you here," Bao said.

Nothing. Poverty, which meant she couldn't afford passage on a merchant ship. Fear: that she would come back, and truly take the measure of her tribunal's devastation.

"But, if you do stay…" Bao shrugged. "Better not spend too much time with Huu Hieu."

"He's family, too," Linh said. She found Bao's serenity uncanny. Where Huu Hieu was a ship waiting to dash into deep space, he was as fixed as the stars, his face impassive, his gaze the distant one of a man who expected nothing more from the world. He spoke little, and didn't express much either. He might have a been a recluse monk already—save, of course, that he was still waiting for his wife to come back, just like Huu Hieu. "There is nothing wrong with my being with him."

"No," Bao said. "But Huu Hieu is a dangerous man to

know, Cousin. Compassion doesn't mean following people into the abyss."

"You mean Quyen won't approve?" The all-powerful, all-knowing Cousin Quyen, the one who thought the whole station was hers to rule, from allowances to hearts and minds?

His face didn't move. "All revelations lead to the Way, but not every revelation must be made in its own time, to people who are ready to receive it."

Buddhist nonsense? "I don't worship the Buddha," she said, more haughtily than she'd meant.

"I know you don't," Bao said, softly. "But think on it, nevertheless."

And he, too, walked away, leaving her to curse at an empty corridor.

"This is the place?" Quyen asked Xuan Rua.

Her niece nodded. "As far as I know, yes." She ran her fingers in her hair, nervously. "Aunt…"

"I know." Quyen shook her head. Here they were, both of them, dressed as young, unmarried women with untied hair, with only the presence of the Honoured Ancestress in her mind.

Quyen felt naked and vulnerable, in more ways than one. It had been years since she'd left the family quarters without an escort or some sort of company. And Xuan Rua, who was too preoccupied by her father's lack of filial piety, was hardly the ideal companion.

But she'd told the Honoured Ancestress she would

retrieve Du Khach's implant, and this hardly meant delegating the task to someone else.

It didn't look like much, as shops went: a little storefront which sold jade ornaments and gold jewellery, mostly displaying trinkets in its window, though the rotating holos hinted at the possibility of other, more valuable pieces. Even through the trance, it came as nothing more than what it appeared to be, utterly unimportant.

Quyen pushed the door, letting the chimes echo in the narrow, dark interior of the place: an affectation, as the Honoured Ancestress had enough power to provide daylight to all dwellings.

A wizened old man was waiting for them by the counter. Though it was early in the day, he was wearing full evening garb: rich robes of silk in the Xuyan fashion, embroidered with peaches and bamboos. No doubt the pattern on the robes referred to a literary citation, or a famous proverb. But Quyen had neither the capacity nor the inclination to decipher what was at best an affectation.

"You are Zhang Pingtou?" she asked.

"I have that honour, yes," Zhang said. His voice was slightly accented, though his Viet was flawless. "What can I do for you, elder sister? I have wedding jewellery…"

Quyen raised a hand. "I have no time for this, younger brother." It wasn't until she saw his shocked face that she realised she'd used her business voice, speaking with the authority of one who managed Prosper Station, rather than a timid young woman.

So much for disguises.

Zhang's face carefully recomposed itself. He looked downwards, betraying reluctant respect. "Lady Quyen."

Quyen was no Lady. That was a title reserved for scholar-officials such as Cousin Linh. But she wasn't about to point that out to him. "I'm told you…" —demons take her, there was no polite way of saying this— "…you offer the opportunity to hear the twittering of sparrows here." She used the Xuyan expression for the opening of the mah-jong game.

Zhang grimaced. It was minute, but Quyen clearly saw it. She wondered whether he'd have the guts to deny her, but he was smarter than that. "Who am I to oppose the meeting of friends, and the sharing of common interests?"

"Friends meeting sometimes leave each other…gifts?" Quyen said, ironically.

She could see his mind working, trying to find the Classic she might be quoting, before he finally realised the allusion was her own. He was too used to working with scholars, with people delighting in wordplays, in obscure references, who weighed their words before speaking or composing a letter. Quyen knew part of that, enough to follow some of her husband's speeches, but not enough to be a scholar. And she was quite happy that way.

"Tell me what you want, Lady Quyen."

"My elder brother played the other night," Quyen said. "And he lost…heavily."

Zhang's gaze did not waver. "No more than usual, I'm afraid," he said.

Somehow, it did not surprise Quyen that Huu Hieu

was useless at mah-jong. "Nevertheless...I'm sure you know all about spending money you do not have."

Zhang's lips quirked, in a minute smile. "Friends do not deny each other money."

And he was proud, no doubt, of being the one who saw to that. In other words, he made sure that no debts remained unpaid. He might even have suggested the... monstrosity of Huu Hieu's selling his own implants.

Quyen forced down the sharp retort in her throat, and said instead, "Friends also do not spend their family's wealth when they can avoid it. You know what I want, Master Zhang."

"The matter is confidential. As you no doubt know. I wouldn't remain long in business if I allowed my friends' names to become public."

"I would keep the strictest confidence," Quyen said, carefully. All she had to do was ask the Honoured Ancestress to scan through who had entered the shop, and to question those people. He had a choice between giving her a single name, or having a dozen of his customers interrogated. But it would have been the height of uncouthness to make the threat explicitly. She picked her words as carefully as scholars wrote memorials, taking care never to make him lose face.

"You are an honourable woman, Lady Quyen." If Zhang was grimacing, he hid it well. "Huu Hieu left with Thien."

"Thien?" Quyen felt a nudge at the edge of her field of vision. When she opened herself up to it all she saw was a single blinking light in one of the middle rings, instead of the detailed biodata and genealogical information on Thien she'd been expecting.

Zhang made a complex gesture with his right hand, between approval and contempt. "Thien won't have, ah, kept what you're looking for, Lady Quyen. I would check with people who might... be in need of blessings?"

The blinking light in Quyen's field of vision resolved itself into a narrow entrance, identical to the standard living units on the station. But then the overlay widened and plunged inwards, revealing a wide courtyard around which were arrayed consoles and writing tables.

"A school," Quyen said. The overlay zoomed out to reveal the name over the courtyard: Abode of Brush Saplings. The needy. Of course. Who would need implants more than the students preparing for the state examinations? "Why this one?" she asked.

Zhang smiled. "You wouldn't know about it, Lady Quyen. It's a school for the mid-rings, neither poor nor wealthy enough to afford a private tutor."

In other words, people who would desperately need to succeed at the examinations in order not to fall back into their parents' poverty. "You're sure?" she asked Zhang.

He nodded, with both hands spread. "Come back to me if you think I guided you falsely."

She hesitated, but it appeared he was telling her the truth. He would have little interest in misleading her. "I'm sure you're a man who can appreciate some of the Emperor's sayings aren't meant for all mortals under Heaven."

Quyen extended a hand, calling on the Honoured Ancestress in her mind to open up a stream where she could extend some minor privilege to him, as price of his silence. A favour for a favour, as the ancients would say.

Nothing happened.

It was as if her mind had gone silent, as if, tottering, she'd reached out for a familiar hand in the dark and found only emptiness. Gasping, she reached out another time. Again and again, her attempts met an invisible wall, a silence deeper than that of the void between the stars, and more frightening.

Through a haze she saw Xuan Rua move towards her, concern etched on every line of her face, her mouth shaping words she couldn't hear; saw Zhang, his face puckered in puzzlement. Everything around her was silent, and she was as lonely as she'd been twenty years ago, disembarking from the ship that had taken her to Prosper Station.

And then, as abruptly as a knife stroke across the throat, the world snapped back into focus. The air around her was greasy, charged with electricity. The familiar tightness filled her chest, the sense that she was small and insignificant, but always cared for.

"Child?" The Honoured Ancestress asked. "What's wrong?"

"Nothing," Quyen said, the lie tasting as acrid as dust on her tongue.

Linh found Quyen in the heartroom, looking upwards with the white of her eyes showing, and her lips moving once in a while. She was no doubt subvocalising with the Honoured Ancestress.

Linh wedged herself against the wall, watching the poem lines run past her across the wall until they all blurred into confused images: cities under moonlight, tribunals where people flocked to see the clear blue of justice spreading over them like the cloak of Heaven. Everything looked whole and unbroken, the buildings so new and radiant that they broke her heart. She felt a pressure against her mind, saw the world take on an oily sheen. Her mouth flooded with an acrid tartness like tamarind. "Honoured Ancestress," she said.

The Honoured Ancestress' touch was light, almost negligible compared to the wave of sickness that had sent Linh to her knees when she'd first arrived on Prosper. "Quyen will be with you in a moment, child. I have let her know you're here."

To Linh's dread, the Honoured Ancestress did not withdraw but merely stood by, waiting. She was a Mind, Linh reminded herself with a shiver. A Mind that could be everywhere in the station, taking into account everyone's preferences and designed environments, and still be there at her core, speaking with several members of the family through her largest interface in the station.

"You're not often here," the Honoured Ancestress said.

"Should I be?" Linh asked. It had been made pretty clear by Quyen that she wasn't a member of the family, and she'd had no desire to join the daily flow of family members paying their respects to the Honoured Ancestress.

A low, thunderous sound Linh realised was a chuckle. "Oh, child. I'm no fool."

Probably not, but she was not human. Borne in a human womb, made by humans, but still…she was not human enough to understand relationships, and feelings. Thank Heaven, for life on Prosper would become unbearable if the Honoured Ancestress literally kept watch over every one of their actions.

"I apologise," Linh said. "I assumed my presence in the morning would be unwelcome."

The Honoured Ancestress said nothing for a while, and appeared distracted. "You do as you wish, child. I do not rule your life."

No, but Quyen thought she did. "I see," Linh said. "Thank you."

The Honoured Ancestress made that strange sound that might have been a laugh, and withdrew, leaving Linh alone, struggling to return to the calm with which she'd entered the heartroom. Truth to tell, the Honoured Ancestress disquieted her; there were no Minds on planets. The only times Linh had been in contact with a Mind had been on the mindship that had brought her to Prosper. It was a faster journey than on any normal vessel, but a deeply unpleasant one.

"Cousin." Quyen had finished her conversation with the Honoured Ancestress, and was walking towards her. "What a surprise to see you here. I hope I did not keep you waiting too long." The sentence was a distracted afterthought. Quyen clearly did not mean any of it, paying lip-service to politeness.

"Not at all," Linh said in the same tone. "I was speaking with the Honoured Ancestress."

"You were?" A flash of something Linh could not identify crossed Quyen's face. Was it anger? Annoyance? "How did She seem to you?"

"What kind of a question is that? I'm not the one used to Prosper," Linh said, more angrily than she'd intended.

"No. Indeed you are not. What do you want? I'm very busy, as you can see."

Not too busy to keep track of Linh, or to send her unwanted advice about who to befriend in the family. Linh bit back the angry reply and said, "I wanted to talk to you."

"You are talking to me." Quyen waved her large sleeves, dismissively. "Tell me what the point of this is."

Linh took a deep breath. "Cousin Quyen, I am not well suited to the post you gave me. Your nieces are both brilliant girls, and they have little need of a tutor to pass the examinations. Even if I were a good teacher..." She spread her hands in a conciliatory gesture. *Gently, child*, First Ancestor Thanh Thuy whispered in her mind. *You must never force a choice upon people.*

Perhaps she should not, but Linh had had more than enough of Quyen's faceless games.

"I see." Quyen's face had gone flat. "You are unsatisfied with the current arrangements, then."

"Yes." Linh could have equivocated, could have been polite, dancing around the facts with the skill of a poet. She didn't.

"You find, perhaps, that they are not good enough for you? That your *achievements*"—Quyen spat the words—"entitle you to more?"

"I can help you," Linh said. "You are flooded with refugees, plagued with supply issues. As a magistrate, I have experience dealing with large amounts of people…"

"As a magistrate." One could have cut ice with Quyen's voice. "High and mighty, sheltering us all like the clear blue of the sky. You'll find that here, such things mean little. This is no planet, and we have no use for scholars. Take what you have been given, and if you're still unsatisfied with it, I advise you to see Magistrate Van, who might give you a better welcome as an agent of the Emperor. But I doubt it. He's as busy as the rest of us."

All magistrates were always busy, but they always made time. The ploy was transparent. Quyen had no intention of helping her. She'd never had any. Linh made a last attempt, struggling to keep her voice even. "It's not Magistrate Van I'm interested in," she said. "The family…"

"Spare me the family," Quyen snapped. "You came to us because we were convenient, but you have no intention of being part of this station."

"I'm trying."

"You're not. The Twenty-Third planet is behind you, cousin. Stop dreaming on what could have been, and focus on your work and your place here. Understand what this is all about. This isn't about running a faceless station, but about dealing with family members."

"I am dealing with them," Linh said, more forcefully

than she'd intended to. "Teaching the girls, as you wished me to."

Quyen snorted. "This is about more than the girls, Cousin. This is about us. About what makes us the way we are, and what problems we face."

"Are you referring to Huu Hieu?" Linh asked.

"Among other things." Quyen didn't even protest that she was having Linh watched for her own good, or attempt to justify herself. She was so certain that she was right, that she knew everything under Heaven. "I have enough problems with wayward family members without you being corrupted by them."

"I'm perfectly capable of defending myself, even if you do turn out to be right about Huu Hieu."

Quyen shook her head, and it was obvious she didn't believe Linh. "You're not very capable, Cousin Linh. You're naive, and not prepared for life aboard Prosper, and show no willingness to listen and learn. Put yourself in a more receptive frame of mind. Then, perhaps, I'll reconsider. When you've proved yourself."

How dare she? She was a mere housewife who had not had the discipline to pass the examinations, who struggled with even the most simple of leadership tasks. How dare she explain to Linh what she could and could not do?

"I've amply proved myself," Linh said, coldly. "I won't perform tricks for you, Cousin."

She could feel Fifth Ancestor Hoang wince in her head. But she didn't need that, didn't need their advice about reconciliation and making no enemies, about peace, and about safeguarding the harmony of the family. There was nothing she could do with Quyen, who was obviously determined to grind Linh into the ground until nothing but dust was left.

Quyen had gone as pale as rice flour and her hands were shaking. Her voice, though, remained perfectly even. "Is that so? Then I think we are done here, cousin." She turned away, back towards the centre of the heart-room, and the Honoured Ancestress' physical presence. Her eyes rolled up a fraction and she went back to her communication with the Mind.

Linh was almost out of the room when Quyen spoke again. "I am reminded by the Honoured Ancestress that, no matter how uncouth and unpleasantly arrogant you might be, you are still family." Every word was pronounced very clearly, with the precision of a pestle pounding against food. "You can stay here. In the light of this, I'll grant you your one wish: you're obviously unsuited for preparing the girls for their examinations. I'll accept your resignation from that, but nothing else. Have a good day, *magistrate*."

Linh left, seething.

"I have an appointment with the teacher of the Abode of Brush Saplings," Xuan Rua said. She poured tea, carefully, into three cups. "Tomorrow, at the Third Bi-Hour, before the students arrive. We'll both go, but I'm not sure…" She paused, staring at the table. "I'm not sure whether he's involved or not."

Quyen sat, watching the dark liquid pool along the translucent, veined porcelain—a painstaking reproduction of celadon from Old Earth, worth perhaps more than the entire station. She inhaled the slow smell of unfurling jasmine flowers. How easy it would be to lose herself in it, to forget about everything that needed her attention. The trance tugged at her: an altercation with the attendants on the refugee levels, three thefts from the noodle-seller stands in the outer rings, a building license for a Buddhist temple two rings away from the Family's quarters...

Everything seemed fine. The Honoured Ancestress was speaking and acting as She always did. But she still remembered what had happened in Zhang's shop; and the earlier lapse, when the Honoured Ancestress had failed to notice Huu Hieu's drunken swagger through the corridors.

Something was wrong. Minds didn't behave that way. They weren't meant to grow old, to change. They weren't meant to fade. But it couldn't be sabotage, no matter how much Quyen might have wished for it. The Honoured Ancestress had inviolable chambers, inaccessible to anyone save a Master of Grand Design Harmony, the makers of Minds, who were all in other orbital habitats, or in the capital on the First Planet.

Something was wrong, and she could think of nothing to do to fix it. She'd sent engineers into the corridors, looking over the system, and they had only confirmed the decline that Quyen had witnessed. But they could offer no cause.

"You're keeping a watch on the school," she said to Xuan Rua. It wasn't a question.

Quyen's brother-in-law Bao reached for one of the cups and cradled it in his large hands like a trapped bird. "We're all helping with that," he said. "Xuan Rua and I."

"And your youngest daughter." Quyen ignored Xuan Rua's wince. Xuan Kiem was only two years younger than Xuan Rua, but she'd always been the darling of her father, and it had spoiled her, narrowing her focus until she could only think of her destiny. It would do her good to be involved in family affairs, but Quyen had no illusion on how painful the whole process would be. "I'll talk to her, if you won't."

Xuan Rua shook his head. "She did help."

Pitifully little, if Quyen was any judge. But she let it slide. Her niece was the least of her worries now. Truth to tell, she would dearly have loved to let Huu Hieu be the least of her worries, let him sink in his own filth. But, even if he were not family, there was the matter of the implants…

"He's involved," Bao said. "He has to be."

"The teacher of the Abode of Brush Saplings?" Xuan Rua sat down, her eyes wandering away from her cup, her whole body tense. "Surely…"

"Teachers in this kind of school are badly paid." Bao's voice was quiet, serene; a fact dispensed by Immortals.

"I set the allowances," Quyen said. "I wouldn't want to think they're unfair."

"It's not about fairness," Bao said. "It's about greed. And I'm not criticising your allowances. You recognise that not everyone is equal, and that there has to be a hierarchy, to remind each and every one of us of our place and duty."

Quyen wondered how much of that was aimed at Huu Hieu.

"What I don't understand is why sell them," Quyen said, slowly. Zhang had sent her the recordings of the mah-jong games, and it had been abundantly clear that, although Huu Hieu was losing, it wasn't a lot of money. With his allowance, he could clearly have paid it all, and still have plenty of money to spare. The sale of the implants had been deliberate, calculated to bring in a large amount of cash.

"He needed money," she added, "but not that much. And it's a dangerous gamble." The Honoured Ancestress monitored all transactions on Prosper Station, except those done within an individual's private home. It was possible to sell the implants, but one would have to be very, very careful, and never generate any anomalies that the Mind could correlate with other facts. To be sure, the price of the implants would be worth the risk. But still…

"My younger brother likes to have his treasures." Bao's voice was a lash.

"I don't think Father is that way." Xuan Rua looked ill at ease. Bao was her uncle, and commanded her respect. But Huu Hieu, as her flesh-and-blood father, always took precedence. "And Aunt Quyen is right. His allowance is large enough to compensate for a thousand such gambling sessions."

"Mmm," Quyen said. So it was either staggeringly *huge* gambling debts—but it hadn't looked that way on the recordings—or it was something else entirely.

She stared at her cup for a while. The liquid was clear and fragrant, but it seemed to shake with the rhythm of the station. Gradually an oily sheen spread over the cup, and a familiar pressure pervaded the room as the walls buckled and groaned. She relaxed, feeling the familiar, comforting presence fill her to bursting.

"Child," the Honoured Ancestress said.

"There is no news of Du Khach's implant." Quyen felt her face flush red. "The three mem-implants seem to be gone from the system. But we'll get them back. I made you a promise, and I'll keep it."

"Of course, child. I have faith in you."

And Quyen wouldn't disappoint Her. The Honoured Ancestress was hardly capricious, never complaining, and seldom asking for things for Herself. Honouring Her request was the very least Quyen could do to repay her. "The whole family is working on it, Honoured Ancestress."

There was a pause, while the pressure in the room seemed to grow even greater. The cup Bao held in his hand seemed to shift, alternating between a metallic sheen and complete transparency. The metal under Quyen shifted and yielded, like quicksand.

"I can provide some help, child. The implants are still within the station. I can feel that much, but I cannot tell where they are."

"Can you tell if they're in use?" Quyen asked.

"They're not," the Honoured Ancestress said. "Or I could find them much more easily. Child, you know I do not monitor everything on Prosper Station."

No, not lately. There was a cold stirring in Quyen's belly. She had limits, and Quyen was genuinely frightened. The Honoured Ancestress was Prosper Station, and she could not afford to falter, or to grow weak.

"You don't have to," she said, more gruffly than she'd intended. "You asked me something, and I'll get it for you. That's all there is to it."

The Honoured Ancestress was silent. Then she spoke in a completely different tone of voice—no longer the wise grandmother's, but a child's, filled with wonder as they watched a kite rise on air-currents for the first time. "Someone is coming."

"Someone?" Quyen rose but before she could let the trance seize her, the Honoured Ancestress was with her, carrying away from the room and the three cups of tea, receding in her mind's eye like the three eyes of some Hindustani god.

She stood in the darkness of space, with only the cold, unblinking light of the stars and the vast, reassuring presence of Prosper Station at her back. A point that seemed like yet another star shifted, and became the prow of a ship headed towards them. It was sleek and smooth, as deadly as the swords of old. Instead of being the standard utilitarian grey metal, it had embossed dragons twining on its hull. The heads of the great beasts met at the prow, and the tails faded away at the back of the ship, so that the dragons seemed to extend themselves into the blackness of space.

Everything about it, from the flowing lines to the five-clawed dragons, screamed official.

Beside Quyen, the Honoured Ancestress spoke, slow and leisurely, and perhaps a little afraid. "*The Carp that Leapt Over the Stream.*"

"It's a state ship," Quyen said. "From the capital."

"From the capital, yes," the Honoured Ancestress said. "But it's private. Registered to Pham Quoc Oanh, a civil official of the Third Rank."

The name meant nothing to her. "Then I don't see…"

Another wrench, and over the stars appeared lines, slowly converging to form the shape of a family tree, tracing a slow ascent from Quyen to the Honoured Ancestress Herself; and then sideways and down, until they'd connected Quyen to Lady Oanh.

Quyen let out a breath she hadn't been aware of holding. "She's…"

"Grand Master of Design Harmony, like her mother and grandmother and great-great-grandmother before her. A shaper of metal and of synthetics; a dreamer of buildings and of wind and water."

A hole was opening in Quyen's belly. "She made Prosper Station."

"Her ancestor," the Honoured Ancestress corrected, but it made no difference. Quyen's ancestor had borne the Honoured Ancestress in her belly; but this Lady Oanh's ancestor had made every nook and cranny of Prosper

Station, shaping the flow of the five elements over the station until the Honoured Ancestress could slip into its structure as easily as into tailored robes.

She made...Quyen stopped. She thought of the chambers of the Honoured Ancestress, the place where Her physical body rested, which would open to no one but a Grand Master of Grand Design Harmony. "Has she given any motive for her presence?"

"She says it is a courtesy visit."

The hollow in Quyen's stomach closed, replaced by a cold sense of purpose, as unsettling as a naked blade. "A courtesy visit?" Three days out in deep spaces from the nearest planet?

The Honoured Ancestress was silent for a while, communing with the vast array of sensors around Prosper Station. "The ship's Mind says that they had business with Felicity Station."

Felicity was their nearest neighbour. After that, it was another four days out to an inhabited planet, one so small that it hadn't yet got a rank in the state classification. Quyen could have asked what Lady Oanh had wanted from Felicity, but it was likely a private matter, if she was on her own ship and not on an imperial craft.

She supposed that, if Lady Oanh had come this far, she might as well detour, and see what her ancestor had made. But still...

"A courtesy visit," she said, aloud, though she didn't need to.

"A banquet," the Honoured Ancestress said. "A private

interview. Gifts. That would be…appropriate." There was still the same disturbing awe in Her tone.

"You want to see her," Quyen said.

The Honoured Ancestress did not speak for a while. "I'm not like you, child. I wasn't haphazardly cobbled together in a womb from the alliance of am and duong. I was made from beginning to end. Designed. And she is a descendant of my maker. A goddess…" Her voice trailed off. She sounded…human. Disturbingly so. Human. Mortal. Finite. All that Prosper could not be.

She…

Quyen thought of their visitor. Lady Oanh. Grand Master of Design Harmony. Maker of space stations, aligner of Minds and hardware. And, what she made, she could diagnose, she could repair.

A favour for a favour…

"A banquet," Quyen repeated. "A proper welcome. Yes, let's give her that. Something large enough for her to look kindly upon us."

Book 2
Lady Oanh

If Linh's arrival had thrown ripples into the family's complacency, Lady Oanh's arrival unleashed a storm. Hordes of attendants passed through the courtyards, carrying everything from baskets of live fowl to bottles of wine—some so dusty they must have dated back to the Exodus, back when there was still a single home planet, and a Dai Viet by the shores of a sea.

In the confusion everyone forgot Linh. Xuan Kiem and Xuan Rua were "recruited", which meant closeted with Cousin Quyen and the rest of the elder generation, planning the spirits knew what. If it was only for a formal dinner menu, Linh could have thought of a few dozen appropriate offerings, depending on Lady Oanh's rank and the actual purpose of her visit. But of course no one thought to ask her. Typical.

Not that she wanted to see Quyen or hear her name, after what had happened in the heartroom. The gall of the woman, dismissing her like some lice-ridden beggar…

In the meantime, she busied herself at the Hall of Network Access, desperately checking her message box. No news from Giap. No news from anyone. She might as well be dead to the world.

She saw Lady Oanh from a distance, bowing down with the rest of the family. She followed her to the heartroom, where she had her interview with the Honoured Ancestress. But other than that, Linh had no wish to interfere with Lady Oanh and retreated into her own quarters, using up her allowance to download vids of Xuyan operas. It was regressive stuff, with only men and gender-changed men allowed on stage. Thankfully, she was able to find some more modern operas, which mimicked the flight of ships in space with localised Mind-interference; creating environments in which the dancers could fly, and adopt positions that would have been impossible in a planetary environment.

On the second day after Lady Oanh's arrival, Linh was using her console to draw a picture of mountains lost in a sea of white clouds, when she suddenly became aware that someone was watching her—a prickling at the nape of her neck, like an intimation of danger.

She raised her eyes, expecting Quyen or possibly Bao, with more moralising about her inappropriate relationship with Huu Hieu and her "regrettable" lack of willingness to become part of the station's life, to bow and scrape the floor before Quyen like everyone else.

But it wasn't Quyen. Instead, she saw a group of attendants in family livery, framing a short, plump woman in an áo dài tunic and trousers. For a moment, Linh couldn't place her, and then she felt the aura of effortless authority radiating from the woman.

Lady Oanh. Third Rank. Linh's practised eye followed the cut of the áo dài, the peacock badge of rank sewn over the heart. Three steps away from the Emperor himself. Every one of the ancestors within her screamed for her to abase herself and she did, kneeling and then bringing her head to touch the ground, feeling the coolness of the station's tiles on her brow.

"We're not in court, child." Lady Oanh's voice was low, with a slight provincial accent. (Second or Third planet, perhaps, though Linh couldn't place the exact location.) "You may rise. There is no need for such formalities. Not between countrymen."

Countrymen? Linh rose, careful to avoid meeting Lady Oanh's gaze. It would have been disrespectful, as well as close to suicide. Lady Oanh was no retired official and she only had to say the word for Linh to be arrested.

She heard an amused laugh. "You don't believe me. But I can assure you, I wasn't always this grand." Her accent had changed, taking on the lilting tones that Linh knew all too well: the accent of Tan Phuoc, which Linh didn't hear outside of family visits.

"You're…"

"From the city of Tan Hoa." Lady Oanh sounded amused. "First child of Fisherman Ma."

It seemed to invite an answer and Linh said, "I'm the first child of Moral Mentor Thi Sac, from Phu Mi."

"Indeed. I was your father's friend."

Linh sucked in a deep, burning breath. Not only was Lady Oanh of the Third Rank, she also ranked close to Linh's own parents, and thus Linh should give her the same respect.

"You honour me by your visit," Linh said. First Ancestor Thanh Thuy was rising in her mind, reminding her of etiquette, suggesting quotes from the Classics that Linh could use to impress Lady Oanh. "Just as you honour this space station."

Lady Oanh laughed: a short, dainty sound which seemed to punch through the air. "Child, I've told you already. No need. Would you believe I'm here for a restful visit?"

Linh did not answer.

"Look at me," Lady Oanh said.

Linh wasn't meant to. First Ancestor Thanh Thuy was hesitating in her mind, but Linh already knew the correct behaviour. If a superior wanted to be treated as an equal, you humoured them, no matter how much this might go against the teachings of Master Kong.

She looked up. The guards had fanned away, leaving her and Lady Oanh in a growing circle of silence. The wind, an affection of the station's Mind, lifted dust and paper leaves from the floor, and the sounds around them seemed oddly muted.

Lady Oanh's face was utterly unremarkable—not that of the princesses of legends, hardly enough to lead entire planets into ruin. But it had the expression of people used to authority, an expression Linh knew all too well, the mirror of her own ancestors' expressions, of Linh's own face. Though lately all she'd seen in the mirror was the lined, haunted face of a powerless exile.

"I'm told," Lady Oanh said, "that you come to us from the Twenty-Third Planet."

How much did she know of Giap, of the memorial? Not enough, surely. News went fast, but if she'd been travelling for the past month? "It was my first posting."

"As district magistrate, I suppose." Lady Oanh's mouth quirked up in the barest hint of a smile. "It's always... enlightening. My own first posting was the Thirty-First planet, much more remote and...provincial than the Twenty-Third."

The Thirty-First Planet, Fifth Ancestor Hoang said, a whisper in Linh's mind. One of the first casualties of the war. The two rebel factions battled over its ownership, and tore it to pieces.

Linh hesitated. What was the proper phrasing to offer regrets, something that wouldn't be too familiar or too distant? First Ancestor Thanh Thuy, for once, seemed at a loss, and before she could suggest something that would inevitably be too formal, Linh said, "This is presumption on my part, but I offer my humble condolences."

Lady Oanh nodded, making no commentary. "It was but a posting, child, and it was long ago. The Twenty-Third Planet's loss no doubt hurts you more."

The loss, yes. But more than that, the fact that she hadn't been there. That she'd run away in fear for her own life, and deserted them. That she couldn't speak to Giap or stop him from taking the war to the rebel armies. "I had people I loved as much as family there."

Lady Oanh nodded. "And here you are, a refugee among strangers."

"Family," Linh said.

Her smile might have been ironic. It was hard to

tell with her weather-beaten face. "The ties of blood are strong, but the strongest ones are between mother and daughter, not between distant cousins."

"Those ties are what we make of them," Linh said. "Are not friends and sworn brothers as important as blood-brothers? A true friend will know your heart, and hear the roar of running waters and the distant wind over the mountains in the song of your zither, without any need for you to speak aloud."

"You must, however, do something for your friends," Lady Oanh said, shaking her head. Perhaps she was amused at the literary reference? "Collect their body and bring it home at your own expense; die on the same hour, same day and same year; all that shows that you value them above all else."

Linh said nothing. She had nothing to do with Prosper anymore, and no desire to wish them well in any way.

She groped for another subject, and found only the trivial. "I imagine your honoured ancestor was proud of this station."

Lady Oanh's face altered, imperceptibly. She hesitated, but then she nodded. "A panther dies and leaves behind its skin; a man dies and leaves behind his words and reputation. A trite but true saying. My ancestor built this station. Every single ring on it, from the centre to the boundary ones. Everything from the heartroom to the emergency ships. And I see her…everywhere."

Which meant she either had access to her ancestor's poetry and writings, or that she had a mem-implant, or both. Which would hardly have been surprising given how far she'd risen in the hierarchy of the Empire. "It's a joy to behold your ancestor's work."

"Perhaps," Lady Oanh said. "Or perhaps it's bittersweet, because I will never know her, never ask her how she composed her space stations, never take her words and work into mine." She made a gesture with her hand, as if opening a fan, or dismissing a troublesome underling. "You haven't asked me about the capital, child."

An icy fist closed around Linh's heart. "Should I have, grandmother?"

"Oh, child." Lady Oanh's gaze focused on Linh, as if trying to extract the truth from a criminal by sheer strength of mind. She wasn't a fool. But of course it would take more than successfully designing a few spaceships or space stations to rise to Third Rank. "Do you truly think I would come here, and not know anything about you? Your memorial has been…noted." Her face had gone impassive again. Any clues about what she might be feeling scattered like the pages of a book with a broken spine.

"I had to write it," Linh said. She wasn't sure why she was telling Lady Oanh. It was Giap who should have heard this, Giap who'd had to think of the consequences of what she'd done. But Giap was…so far away he might as well have been on another planet. Giap was blind, deaf and unable to see the danger around him. "The Great Virtue Emperor's conduct of the war…"

"… has been weak, and unsuited to a Son of Heaven. The unity among us should be paramount, rather than the preservation of our lands." Lady Oanh's face was serene. "I read the memorial."

Of course she would have and of course she would not commit herself. Scholars had been executed for saying the wrong thing, even at the right time. "What of the court, then?"

"The court…is in flux," Lady Oanh said. "The Great Virtue Emperor has been challenged by his Great Secretary and his ministers; he is urged to show the virtue necessary to uphold the Rong dynasty, to establish proper defences in the outlying planets and chastise the rebelling lords who think themselves clever enough to challenge his dominion."

"I see," Linh said, slowly, though she didn't, not yet. "And the Son of Heaven…"

"The Great Virtue Emperor is young, and eager to prove himself." Lady Oanh shrugged. "And he naturally thinks he shouldn't be given orders by his advisors, as if he were still an immature child."

Which wasn't good. Linh's memorial was all but in line with the ministers and the Great Secretary, and she was nowhere as untouchable as they were. "You have read my memorial."

Lady Oanh's eyes drifted away from her. "Some… sycophants campaign for your removal as magistrate, and for proper chastisement."

Proper. Linh narrowed her eyes. "Is the charge treason against the Dragon Throne?" she asked, praying all the while the answer would be no. One of the Ten

Abominations, the one that would punish, not only the offender or his closest kin, but would extend from line of decent to line of descent, across the entirety of her lineage, sparing nothing and no one...

"I don't know." Lady Oanh's eyes transfixed her, as surely as a thrown spear. "It would be, if an edict had been signed, or even drafted."

"But still..." Still it was a risk, and that was the extent of Lady Oanh's warning: that the edict would pass and when it did, every one of Linh's cousins ran the risk of sharing her fate, if they were proved to still have ties with her. If, say, they'd welcomed her as a refugee. And it went up to the ninth generation, which might have been everyone who shared a drop of blood with her.

And Prosper...Prosper's founder shared an ancestor with Linh, and almost everyone here was her distant relative.

Up to the ninth generation. The entire station, wiped from the world.

Linh swallowed, thinking of the garrotte passed around her neck, as surely as that of the executioner. "I could retract, but it would be too late, wouldn't it?"

"Would you truly retract?" Lady Oanh's eyes were emotionless.

Linh felt something cold and hard within her stomach, like an ice-covered stone. "No. I meant every word, and I'll not take them back. We should be strong, rather than fighting among ourselves."

"Of course. Your behaviour does you credit, even if

it augurs little for your life expectancy. Your fate, I fear, rests in the hands of the court."

"I see," she said. "Thank you for your wisdom, Lady Oanh."

Lady Oanh recalled her escort with a snap of her fingers, and headed towards the exit to the courtyard, bathed in Prosper's sickly light. She was halfway there when she turned, as if struck by a wayward thought, although Linh was starting to suspect Lady Oanh never did anything wayward. "Remember the tales about running from death, child?"

The old ones, the ones that said lives ruled by fear were worse than useless, that one should embrace one's duty, one's family...

"Yes," Linh said. Her throat was dry.

"Those who fear death find it on their path," Lady Oanh said. "Your memorial was sensible. Indeed, some would say it pointed to the only way forward the Empire can take. You are not without allies, even in the court itself. Remember this."

Allies. Would it be enough to save her? To save Prosper? Linh tore herself from visions of the Embroidered Guard at her door to bow to Lady Oanh. The official, after all, had all but declared herself on her side.

"I see. Thank you, Honoured Oanh." No matter how grateful Linh tried to sound, the words tasted like dust on her tongue.

Quyen found Xuan Rua in the kitchens amidst an army of attendants carrying everything from live fowls to husked rice. Her niece looked overwhelmed by the sheer mass of people, her face pale in the heat of the cooking units.

Next to her was Hanh, the overseer of the fish sauce vats: a plump, middle-aged woman who always wore a brocade áo dài tunic, no matter the circumstances, as if every event in life required pomp and respect. She bowed to Quyen. "Cousin." The connection was tenuous, third generation, but even without the help of the trance Quyen could place her easily enough.

"Let me guess," Quyen said, after the usual exchange of courtesies. "You're providing your best, but that's all we have."

Xuan Rua grimaced, but did not contradict Quyen, either overtly or subtly. "Prosper Station will live up to its name at least."

Fish sauce was the heart's blood of food, the ingredient that lifted even simple rice to the level of Heavenly meals. Prosper's fish sauce, fermented in huge vats under the light of Red Turtle Star, was legendary, its aroma subtle and understated, revealing the richness of its successive pressings, with the pungent hint of flavour. No other station had a production to rival it. But fish sauce alone did not make a banquet.

"Show me the courses," Quyen said.

Xuan Rua grimaced. "We can make six appetisers, but only a little of each. Silky pork, fried rolls, rolled cakes…" She bit her lip. The rolled cakes were rice flour and hardly suitable for a banquet, and six dishes was pitifully few to entertain an official. Lady Oanh probably was used to ten or twelve courses to open a banquet.

Overseer Hanh barked a short, unamused laugh. "We have enough rice, too, if nothing else."

"At least that's something." Quyen sighed, massaging her forehead, wishing for simpler answers, for a time where her only worry had been the symbolism of the various dishes and whether they would inadvertently offend the guest of honour, rather than whatever they could scrounge from their diminished supplies.

Xuan Rua was moving to the stir-fries, mostly the fish raised in Hanh's spare vats; and pork, the beasts having shown a supernatural ability to breed in space. Then to the soup, a concoction of bitter melon wishing unhappiness away (how Quyen wished it were true); and then pork braised in the milk of coconut from their dwindling orchards, and dish upon dish, each more diminished than the rest, before the final serving of fruit that would conclude the meat—pitayas and lychees and pineapples from the station's orchards.

Quyen sighed. It was all…less than it should have been, small and shrunken, but she couldn't blame Xuan Rua or Overseer Hanh for any of it.

"And the main dish?" Quyen asked.

"Pineapple duck," Xuan Rua said. "It looks dignified even though it's hardly a festival dish, and…"

Quyen raised a hand to stop her. "Duck won't do." Oanh's name meant "nightingale" and it would hardly do to serve up a bird as the main dish. "Can you do something with fish?"

Xuan Rua hesitated. Quyen suddenly remembered how

young she was, not of age to pass the examinations or marry, and even less suitable for being in charge of something this large. Quyen felt it was her fault. She shouldn't have pushed her niece this hard, even if she was swamped by other matters. "Fish in caramel sauce," she said. "Served whole. It should be suitable."

Overseer Hanh grimaced. "It's not much."

Quyen knew that it wasn't, knew all too well that this was like a dying man's last struggle…But no, Prosper wasn't dying, merely going through an illness. When the war was over, it would be different, when her husband Anh was there once more, lending his reassuring solidity to Prosper.

She had to believe that or she might as well ask the Honoured Ancestress to open a hatch for her into deep space, to step through it and be torn apart in an environment never meant for man.

She groped for the trance, found it there, but quiescent, as if the Honoured Ancestress' attention were elsewhere. She could catch a hint of anger, of confusion, like a distant storm. She was still with them, and Lady Oanh would know what to do to help, would make everything right again.

Quyen stared again at the courses in her mind. Everything they could provide, from the lemongrass beef with rice noodles to the salad rolls with pork skin; and knew for a cold, hard fact that Overseer Hanh was right. It wouldn't be enough. Oh, to be sure, it would satisfy Lady Oanh, but not impress her so much that she would accede to unexpected favours. They needed more, and they didn't have it.

Her gaze roamed over the chaos of the kitchen. The head cook Nhu was mixing dipping sauce, the aroma of fish sauce and lime thick around her. Her assistants, Hoang Be and Thanh Hoa, were cutting pork in thin slices. The smells that rose reminded her of other banquets, in the distant past: Bao smiling at one of her husband's jests; Huu Hieu declaiming a drunken poem to his wife; all of them together as a flesh-and-blood family, not as a collection of absences and holograms on the ancestral altars. She'd have wept if she was a weaker woman, but weeping had never brought anything or anyone back.

They could not provide more food. Overseer Hanh had made it abundantly clear, and Quyen wouldn't offend her by accessing the trance to check the state of their storehouses. They could not create more elaborate dishes without food, but a banquet wasn't only about food. There had been other attractions in past times: watercolours done before the guest of honour, calligraphy painted on the spot and hung in the hall, poetry composed for the occasion...

Quyen felt the realisation settle in her stomach, a cold, heavy stone over a grave.

For all of this—for *any* of this—they were going to need Cousin Linh's help.

Quyen took Xuan Rua with her. Not because she thought she would be needed, but because she wanted someone else when she faced Linh. When she abased herself.

She had no shame about what she'd told Linh earlier. Even magistrates shouldn't be entitled to such arrogance, and it was Linh's own fault if she could not take what was offered gracefully. Given the circumstances, and the angry way in which the request—no, the *demand*—had been made, Quyen had been fully within her rights to refuse her.

But if it took an abject apology to help the Honoured Ancestress, then Quyen would make it. Anything, as long as it helped keep Prosper safe. As long as it kept the Honoured Ancestress with them.

They found Linh in the courtyard, her eyes closed. She was within the trance, mouthing incomprehensible words. Though the trance would have informed her of their presence, she remained oblivious to them for several moments. By then, Xuan Rua was looking distinctly uncomfortable.

Quyen kept herself calm by reviewing everything that needed her attention. She was to see the teacher of the Abode of Brush Saplings, the one who might well have the missing mem-implants, early on the following morning, before the banquet, which would mean more delegation of tasks to Xuan Rua and Overseer Hanh. It left her nervous. Neither of the two women were well suited for managing the myriad emergencies that were bound to appear in the last moments before the banquet: missing ingredients, equipment that wasn't functioning, all the many things that required a firm hand and a quick mind. Overseer Hanh didn't have the imagination, and Xuan Rua didn't have the confidence.

She could feel the trance, fluttering in her grasp, and only yesterday the Honoured Ancestress had spoken to her, asking Quyen if she'd felt that anything was wrong on board the station. Quyen had lied. She had said everything was fine, that the banquet would be unforgettable, as it had been designed to be.

"You are kind, child," the Honoured Ancestress had said. "But...I feel it. I know that..." She'd paused then, and the silence had seemed too stretch on forever, pregnant with a thousand cancerous growths. "I've had absences. I've felt myself go. You can't pretend everything is as it should be."

"It doesn't matter." Quyen had shaken her head. "We'll have you well. I promise." As she'd promised to recover Du Khach's implant—a task at which she'd failed so far.

"Make me well?" The Honoured Ancestress had asked. "I hold the lives of everyone aboard Prosper. I can't afford to be less than fully efficient."

"I promise," Quyen had said again.

The Honoured Ancestress had not answered, but Quyen had known She wasn't convinced. That She was afraid, not even for herself, but for Her children, and all the people aboard Prosper. And Quyen felt her heart break all over again. She'd find a way to make everything right. She had to.

"Cousin. Niece. Be welcome to my humble abode." Linh had turned towards them, though she did not bow, or made any pretence of more than mere civility. "Can I offer you anything to drink or eat?"

Quyen rose, taking a deep breath to steady herself. Linh's scorn was almost palpable, like a blistering wind in the deep spaces. "I have come to apologise for my earlier outburst. It was uncalled for."

"Indeed." Linh did not look surprised. Quyen fully knew that she'd ask what favour Quyen wanted within a few heartbeats. To forestall this, she said, "We have an urgent family affair to take care of. Missing mem-implants."

"I see." Linh's expression did not move. She looked like any magistrate on her dais, her gaze utterly neutral, face revealing nothing of what she felt.

"They are our own ancestors," Quyen said. "Dear to the Honoured Ancestress and to us."

"A rather distressing setback." Linh's face was still expressionless, but she appeared marginally less cold. "I can well understand how you feel. To have strangers in possession of your family's treasures…"

"Yes, exactly. You can see how preoccupying the situation is."

"And this is what you want my help for?" Linh sounded wary, but excited. Always so ready to meddle into the station's affairs, even as she refused to take part in its daily life.

"No," Quyen snapped, and then corrected herself. "Not yet." She shouldn't discard possibilities so easily, no matter how much she might loathe Linh. "But I do need your help."

"How surprising." Linh didn't move, or turn away.

Quyen went on, "Prosper is putting on a feast for Lady Oanh, and we want her to remember it as the highlight of her travels." She did not say why. Enough sharing of secrets with an outsider. "For that, we need something memorable. Poetry, perhaps, or calligraphy. You would know better than I."

"Yes." Linh looked at the shadows spreading over the courtyard, extinguishing the light and making it into a mass of rivets and metal, instead of the carefully crafted garden the Honoured Ancestress' systems usually displayed. "Is this payment for sheltering me?"

"No," Quyen said, though she dearly would have loved to nod. "A favour, from a cousin to a cousin." She swallowed, feeling the acrid taste on her tongue. They had no greater spouses left anywhere on Prosper. The only one who vaguely qualified was Huu Hieu, who fancied himself a poet and a scholar in spite of his dismal lack of talents in so many areas of his life. But demons drag her into the Courts of Hell before she bent her back to Huu Hieu.

"I know your poetry would be great," Quyen said, "that it would charm Lady Oanh. This is what your talent is for." And where Quyen's talent would never be: nothing she would ever be honoured for, or remembered for as the ages passed and the memory of her faded from the world, unrecorded in any mem-implants.

"Please, Master Linh," Xuan Rua said. Quyen jerked in surprise. Xuan Rua hadn't said a word for the entire interview. "It would mean much to us." Xuan Rua got up, and knelt on the stones of the courtyard, her head touching the floor, as if Linh were a much-higher ranked official than a mere provincial magistrate.

Linh's gaze did not move, but Quyen thought she looked embarrassed. "Get up, child. I'll think on it, but I'll promise nothing."

Quyen bowed, not as low as Xuan Rua, but low enough to make it clear she recognised Linh's superiority. "We'll await your answer, Cousin."

She'd done all she could. Now it was in the hands of the gods, and of her ancestors.

On the morning after Lady Oanh's arrival, Linh was writing poetry when a knock at the door made her look up.

It was Huu Hieu, looking almost presentable, with his hair neatly brought back into an elegant bun, stabbed with silver pins in the shape of a phoenix wrapped around a star. No, not presentable...

Domestic, she considered, and thought uneasily of caged things: pet birds, ships on display at the docks that would never fly again.

He'd brought fruit which he laid on the table. The pink spikes of pitaya mingled with a few bunches of a yellow fruit she didn't recognise: some kind of longan, though with far smoother skin.

"From the orchards," he said, sheepishly. He looked embarrassed. Had his brother-in-law, Bao, warned him against seeing her?

"I'm glad you decided to take advantage of my offer,"

she said, ignoring the howling of all six ancestors in her mem-implants.

Huu Hieu sat cross-legged in front of the low table; one swipe of his fingers called up a display which hung, trembling, waiting for her to fill it. He sat well away from her, his stance tense. But the tension wasn't sexual, merely the usual unease of a stranger with another stranger.

"Have you heard news from your home planet?" he asked.

Linh shrugged. "Insofar as it's my home. The Twenty-Third Planet was just my first posting."

"But you miss it."

Cousin Quyen was wrong about him. He was sharp, more observant than most people would give him credit for. She guessed that a lifetime with nothing much to do had honed his senses.

"I had friends there, and a life." She didn't say she had none of this here, and he wasn't churlish enough to bring it up. "We had a poetry circle. The Crab Flower Club, which isn't a terribly original name, but we had such talent..." It had been Giap's idea, though he was an indifferent poet at best, making stiff and graceless compositions when his turn came.

She thought of long afternoons under the red sun, watching the clouds drift across the face of the sky; of voices raised in laughter, bowls clinked together as they were refilled with wine; of prompts drawn from official hats, and poems written in the glow of rice alcohol. All that she'd run away from, all that the war had swallowed and crunched to dust within its maw. "Yes. I miss it."

Huu Hieu said nothing, only handed her a fruit, its

skin split open to reveal plump, translucent flesh through which the stone shone like the pupil of an eye. He watched her eat it; then took another one.

"Where were you born?" she asked.

"Far away. Before I was here, I came from Longevity Station."

The network of alliances. She remembered reading about it on her way to Prosper Station, but it hadn't been such a cold reality then. "You were bartered away."

Huu Hieu looked away from her, as if acknowledging for the first time that he was her inferior. "I failed the examinations twice. On the stations, this means only one thing."

Unfit for official life; doomed to be the lesser partner in a marriage, Fifth Ancestor Hoanh whispered in Linh's mind, though really, she'd have guessed that without his help. The rules weren't the same on the planets: more forgiving, but then the planets weren't on such limited resources. "And so you came here."

"Yes." Huu Hieu picked another longan, dug his nails into the skin to split it apart. "It wasn't so bad at first, when my wife was still here. But then..."

But then Quyen had taken over. "I see." With a swipe of her fingers, Linh called up a book of poetry from her personal library. "Shall we read together?"

Huu Hieu nodded. For a while, there was nothing but the slow hum of the holo-screen, a sound that grew until it absorbed them all, and poetry sang in their minds, am and duong verses mingling with each other like the breath of the dragon that was the universe.

"Those are beautiful," Huu Hieu said.

"They are." Linh shook her head. "A pity the poets were never recognised by the literary circles of the capital."

They chatted a bit, about the powerful images: the starships in flight over waterfalls, scattering to other planets like wild geese fleeing the winter; the wine warm in the cups, defying the emptiness of space; the paths of friends crossing only through deep-space travel, in one sense standing together, in the other so apart they might have been in different universes.

Huu Hieu was fidgeting, looking upwards at the dome of the station. His face was pale, pinched in worry, but a feverish energy underlined his gestures. "Has something happened to you?" Linh asked. She picked another book, the annals of Dai Viet dating back to the Lê dynasty, but she didn't display it on the screen yet.

"No." Huu Hieu looked up again at the dome, and shrugged, as if to say it didn't matter anymore. "She's probably listening."

"Who?"

"Who else? The Honoured Ancestress." He spat the word like a rotten lychee. "She who watches over us all."

"You don't approve." She was always stating the obvious.

Huu Hieu hugged himself. "Always watching," he whispered. "Always able to come to you without warning, to press against your mind as though she owned everything..." He looked again at the dome. "Who cares? I'm leaving."

"You are?" That stopped her, like a knife, thrown into

her chest with unerring accuracy, her hand halfway to the table in order to call up more books. "You…"

There was silence for a while, as if they waited for the executioner's sword to fall. Linh broke it, again. "I hadn't thought…" she stopped then, unsure of what he was ready to tell her. Surely he would want it discussed as little as possible?

"There is someone else." Huu Hieu shrugged. Bright, careless, his face tight with desperation, or happiness, she wasn't sure. "On Longevity Station. A girl I once knew who never forgot about me. I never forgot her, either, and now her husband is dead…" He stopped; his eyes strangely bright and feverish.

"Your wife…" Linh said, carefully, as if each word would topple the edifice.

"It's been five years, and my wife hasn't come back. I won't spend my entire life waiting for her. I can't. Don't you see?" Pleading. What could she tell him? She wasn't here to pass judgment, or even to offer advice.

"I'm not family."

"Nonsense. Quyen might not see it that way, but you're as much part of us as Bao or any of my sisters-in-law."

And was the thrill that ran through her joy, or the feeling of the knife sinking deeper into flesh? "So…" she pointed at the fruit. "A parting gift, then."

Huu Hieu's face fell. "They're a gift. Because I visited you, and read your poetry. Don't think of it in terms of parting, please." He looked at the sky again, biting his lip. "It would be best…"

"Absolutely." Linh picked a pitaya, toying with its weight,

careful never to bruise the fruit beneath the skin. "Still, I'm happy for you." And yet…there was an odd twist in her stomach. If he went away, if he escaped Prosper, he'd have his freedom once again. He'd enjoy the company of his lover, of friends and allies, while she would remain on the station, kinless and powerless and isolated. She quenched the thought before it could turn into bitter jealousy. "Shall we return to the poetry then?"

"Tell you what." The feverishness was back in Huu Hieu's eyes. She was reminded again of a man awaiting the plunge into deep space, steeling himself for what was to come. "Let's write poems."

Linh drew in a shaking breath. She'd written nothing since leaving the Twenty-Third Planet. "Why not?" She struggled to keep her voice calm. "You suggested it. Pick a prompt."

"Use the following words: Chrysanthemum. Spaceship. Prosper. In Two Seven style." Huu Hieu's smile was deeply ironic.

"As you wish." Linh bent down, already thinking of words that would fit, of soft and stressed syllables, of the music of the words putting themselves together, allusions to other, older texts playing against each other…

She looked up, vaguely disquieted. Something was wrong, something in the silence of the room, some blinking light in the corner of her vision. But before she could articulate the thought, the presence rose, overlaying the walls with a shimmer like sunlight on algae fields, and Linh's hands tightened, even as she struggled to speak.

She'd expected the Honoured Ancestress but, instead, the scene around her slowly faded to be replaced by a verdant hillside under an intense blue sky. Everything, from the river to the clouds, was riven through with cracks, like torn cloth that revealed the darkness and emptiness between the stars. Linh raised her eyes and saw skeletal birds winging their way through the sky, their cries the forlorn ones of geese.

"Honoured Ancestress?" Linh asked. The Honoured Ancestress did not answer. Instead, a light blinked on the lower left hand corner of her field of vision, the same light that denoted an urgent message, usually from the station's administrator. Linh reached out towards it and it fractured, the letters of its header slowly spreading past her until they had felt burnt into her eye-sockets.

The message had been routed from Felicity, but it had been come from the Twenty-Third Planet. Its trajectory through space had been erratic, leaping from one mindship to another in attempts to leave the cut-off war-zones and return to the planets held by the Empire. It was from Giap, but the seal on it was the two wolves of Lord Soi's banners.

The environment around her fluttered between the verdant hills and the deeper darkness beneath them. Linh opened it, and Giap blinked into existence, not a flat image like his first image, but a full holographic recording, giving him the air of a ghost.

"Magistrate. I apologise, for it would seem I have been unworthy of your faith." He smiled at her, his face wan and drawn. His hair had been pulled into a neat top-knot, and his clothes were the rough, off-white of mourning. Around his neck was a placard, on which was written in red ink his full name and a list of crimes. Linh read the larger letters: "Rebellion against the Celestial Order". He wore the placard and clothes of a condemned man, being led to his execution.

No. The thought was a knife drawn across Linh's throat. Had he not received her message? Had he not...

"As is customary, I have written my last messages, and saved this one for you. I'm no poet, and don't expect you to remember my words beyond what custom dictates." He smiled at her then, and it broke her heart all over again. "Don't blame yourself for what happened. I bear the responsibility of my advice to you, and of what I did after the fall of the province. Be kind, Magistrate. Be strong. But you know all of this already. I was proud to know you, and if my ancestors grant me a place among them, I shall continue to watch over you as I have always done."

Linh reached out, to touch the ghostly hands, but the message was finished, and Giap had blinked out of existence. "Giap!" she called, knowing it was too late already. The rest of the message streamed by her. Under the seal of Lord Soi was the order for Giap's execution, and for the execution of other names she'd known in another lifetime: Chau and his meat dumplings and poetry that never made sense; Van and his dreams of being a soldier in some far-away land; Lan and her effortless, flowing verses that seared the soul, a great talent wasted on a lesser spouse with no ambitions beyond her hearth...

Her entire poetry club, wiped out of existence with a casual note that they had been rebels against Lord Soi's new order. All of it tossed at her like a piece of offal.

"Honoured Ancestress!" Linh screamed. "Show yourself!"

The land around her flickered and tore, and she was back in the courtyard, struggling to breathe. "Child?" the Honoured Ancestress sounded scared. "Something happened…"

"You gave me a *message.*" Linh struggled to pull herself upright, to be stern, unbending, as a magistrate should be. But she couldn't seem to muster the strength to stand up.

Breathe. Breathe, Linh. You have to breathe. One cannot let the dead destroy you. One cannot weep for subordinates. He only did his duty…He wasn't a subordinate, he was a friend, and you should mourn him accordingly… He was to her as Quan Vu to Luu Bi: a sworn brother, and his death is like her own…. Within her, the six ancestors in their mem-implants shouted at each other, a storm of contradictory advice that threatened to tear her apart.

Breathe, Linh, breathe.

Weep.

"I apologise. A malfunction appears to have emptied my priority buffers," the Honoured Ancestress said. There was a pause; then, "Your message had been set aside when Lady Oanh's ship arrived."

"Set aside?"

The Honoured Ancestress stopped and said nothing.

"Set aside by whom?" Linh asked, though she knew

the answer. She'd crushed one of the pitayas. Her fingers were coated in white, sticky flesh which clung to her skin, like guilt, like blood.

"Quyen," the Honoured Ancestress said. "She thought you should hear about this when you were in the right frame of mind. But you don't understand, child. There is something…"

Quyen. Of course. Who else would keep news of the Twenty-Third Planet from her? *Focus on your work and your place here, Cousin. Stop dream about what could have been. Then, perhaps, I will reconsider.* "There is nothing," Linh snapped. "Go away and leave me alone."

Were this Quyen, she'd have snapped, said something about being older and wiser than Linh. But the Honoured Ancestress merely said, in a voice that quivered, "I'm sorry," and the pressure of Her presence faded, leaving Linh alone with Huu Hieu.

Her cousin stared at her; he looked pale. "Cousin. What happened?"

"You didn't see anything, did you?" Linh's stomach contracted into knots. Bad enough to be weak, but that he should see it…

"I…had a message." He forced a smile. "From Longevity. You?"

Another message Quyen had been holding on to, so she could see what they were doing? "A message I had been waiting for a while," she said. "I am well." She forced herself to smile through the lie, until her jawbones hurt with the effort.

She thought of Quyen, of the contrite way she'd apologised for her shortcomings earlier. To think that Linh had almost believed her, that she'd almost agreed to be her dupe once again. And all the while Quyen had been watching incoming messages, making decisions about what Linh could and could not do, had been ruling her life as she ruled everyone else's.

And she had the gall to hope for Linh to exalt Prosper in the eyes of Lady Oanh, to participate in the glorification of Quyen's own petty concerns. She had the nerve to come and see Linh, and dangle mysteries in front of her, to promise that she could be included in family matters, help the station with her skills. She had the nerve to ask through a tangle of lies, and to use Xuan Rua to soften Linh's heart.

She'd been a fool.

"A poem," she said aloud, heedless of Huu Hieu's puzzled stare. Quyen wanted a poem? Linh would give her something that no one aboard Prosper would ever forget.

Quyen had expected Lê Anh Tu to be a portly man. But he was as skinny as a beggar, his face gaunt, almost malnourished, so creased and skeletal that Quyen almost turned to the Honoured Ancestress to ask Her about Tu's allowance. But of course it was foolishness. No one went hungry on Prosper.

The trance flared to life within Quyen, reminded her that Tu was a distant relative, descended from a brother of Quyen's great-grandfather. It mattered little, in truth.

Everyone on Prosper was related to some degree or another. But Quyen took it as a good sign. The trance was working, albeit erratically. The Honoured Ancestress was still with them.

For a while, if nothing else.

The Abode of Brush Saplings was set around a wide, airy courtyard. Its trees and carp-filled basin almost disguised the fact that it wasn't in the open air, but under the subdued lights of Prosper. A gaggle of a dozen students—eight girls, five boys, their ages ranging from five to fifteen—watched Quyen and Tu stroll through the courtyard, the books on their tables forgotten in the rush of curiosity.

How Quyen wished for Xuan Rua. But one of them had to remain in charge of the banquet preparation and this, this interview with Lê Anh Tu, was too sensitive to be left to her niece alone.

Tu said, "I'm honoured by your visit, Mistress Quyen."

Quyen heard the "but" he wasn't saying. "Family matters bring me to you, Master Tu."

He raised an eyebrow, signifying, very clearly, that he might have been family once, but didn't count as such anymore. "We are far away from the Inner Quarters," Tu said. A careful overture, calculated not to cause offence.

"Indeed. But things blow where the wind wills them," Quyen said.

Tu was smarter than Zhang. Indeed, Quyen had the feeling that he knew all of her failures, all the books spread out on his students' tables: writing that she could decipher but not understand. He did not bother to quest for an allusion she could have made, and merely nodded. "You seek the wind's trail, Mistress Quyen."

"It always blows here, doesn't it?" Quyen said, with a flourish of her hands. "Into the middle rings. Far from the warmth of the Honoured Ancestress, but not so far that you feel the cold of space." She hesitated, but she'd lost enough time as it was. There were more pressing concerns, the dinner with Lady Oanh, the war encroaching on them...

She'd have grasped for the Honoured Ancestress, to support her in her moment of need, but she was...afraid of what would happen, should she reach for Her and not find Her anywhere. "And some things, like blown maple leaves, find their way into the most unlikely places."

Tu raised a perfectly manicured eyebrow. He appeared amused, but not unduly surprised. "I have no idea what you're talking about, Mistress Quyen." In his mouth, the "Mistress" appeared almost perfunctory.

Quyen turned her gaze towards the students, who were still watching them from afar. "Your students are bright," she said, keeping her voice low. She would make her point without shaming the children.

"They wouldn't be here otherwise." Was that pride in his voice, or something else entirely? She didn't know what vagaries of life's currents had brought him here in the middle rings. As a tutor to the wealthy, he could have had a much larger allowance. Was it ideals or lack of skills which kept him where he was?

"Our Empire takes talent and knowledge where it can

find it," Quyen said, slowly. "Raising up carps to be dragons. But not all are so fortunate."

"It's not fortune." Tu's hands had tightened, so strongly they shone as white as ceruse. "You and I both know it, Mistress Quyen."

"True." She inclined her head. "It's hard work. Nights of studying the Classics by the dimmed light of Our Honoured Ancestress, of memorising the proper words and citations. It's a good teacher who will guide through the complexities of the eight-part dissertation and the Two-Seven poetry. But all of that comes with wealth. How can one study if one has no spare time? And how can one find a good teacher if one does not pay for them?"

Tu blanched, and his eyes narrowed in anger. An idealist, then. She didn't like that. She'd have few holds on a man like this. "You're suggesting my students will fail."

Quyen inclined her head, gracefully. "I'm suggesting your students are at a disadvantage. Which you already know. You're clever, Tu."

"And you're quick to judge." Tu glanced towards his students. "Flowers don't bloom by themselves, Lady Quyen. They require... care." Quyen smiled, catching the hint. He wanted her to get to the point, so he could get back to his neglected pupils.

"Your students' ancestors were from the outer rings," she said. "Menials for the most part, with thinned blood. To their descendants they gift blessings, and luck, and happiness. But not, sadly, knowledge."

Tu said nothing.

Fine. She would take the story to its end, then, propriety or not. If it was a choice between losing face now and standing, day after day, before the ancestral altar with the shame of having failed the Honoured Ancestress and her own ancestors, Quyen knew exactly what she would choose.

"Knowledge can be given away, from ancestor to child," Quyen said. "Or it can be…stolen."

"Indeed." Tu's voice was flat, his face as blank as a console screen.

"I'm told you're friends with a man named Thien." Quyen raised a hand to forestall his objections. "It's hardly a secret."

"No." Tu smiled, his lips as thin as a knife's blade. "Thien comes often. He understands what it means to seek knowledge."

"As you do?" Quyen raised an eyebrow.

Tu was looking straight at her, like an equal, like a superior, as if he knew all that she could and couldn't do, and didn't care. "As you said, I am a clever man. I know all that it takes for a carp to leap the dragon waterfalls, and if a nudge is needed, then I will give it." His hands were shaking, a slight tremor. "Whatever it takes to make them rise, I will do. Those who grow wise by learning are among the best, and will rise high in society, as you well know. You don't understand, Mistress Quyen, what it is to be poor, to be desperate."

"No one is poor on Prosper," Quyen said, not knowing what else she could tell him.

Tu smiled. "The beautiful thing about poverty is that it

only exists compared to others. True, no one goes hungry on Prosper." He smiled at that, as if he knew exactly what she was doing, the knife's edge that currently separated them from ruin and starvation. "But some are richer than others. Some hand out allowances." He smiled at her, again, a thoroughly unpleasant expression. "Some fly away to other planets, to serve the Dragon Throne. Some have dozens of citizens, to see to their needs, while others have just enough to eat, and to drink themselves insensate in front of their holograms."

"You want us all to be equal?" Quyen shook her head. "You know that's impossible."

"Of course." Tuyen bowed his head. "I merely want...a chance. An opportunity, for the poor to become the wealthy, to receive the five blessings. I know all about hunger."

"I see." Quyen bowed her head, though she didn't understand him at all. The light in his eyes made her deeply uneasy; it was that of a fanatic, far removed from propriety and balance. "So, you and the venerable Thien hold the same opinions on many things." She forced her voice to remain quiet. "On hunger, and equality, and theft."

The word fell in the silence of the courtyard, spread its ripples around the room. In other circumstances, Quyen would have thought the Honoured Ancestress was here, manipulating soundwaves for better effect. But she could feel nothing, not even the trance, as if everything had dropped away from her unexpectedly.

Tu shook his head. "Suspicions are unhealthy, Mistress Quyen."

"Allow me to entertain them, nevertheless."

Tu smiled. "You are free to think what you want. Aren't we all?" He smiled again, and it was a terrible thing, bright and fevered and unhealthy. "But, without proof, you won't go far."

"There are other ways." The words came out of her, torn without conscious volition. Persuasion and torture, and all the planet-side ways that Linh would be so familiar with…

What was she thinking of? This was Prosper, not a planet mired in the dark ages. This was a place of freedom, away from the gaze of the Dai Viet Empire, where the Honoured Ancestress made her own laws. Where a descendant of Lê Thi Phuoc might be poor, might live in the middle rings, but could not be handled with anything other than respect. Blood to blood; flesh to flesh; features to features.

"Of course there are," Tu said, and she knew, they both knew she couldn't, wouldn't use them without utterly shattering Prosper. And another, shameful thought: Huu Hieu wasn't worth it.

"Was that all, Mistress Quyen?" Tu asked. He drew himself up. He was the respected teacher once again, with no trace of the fanatic, or of the gloating thief.

She knew—they both knew—he had the implants. But until she found out where he'd hidden them, there was nothing she could do about it.

"No, that wasn't all." The words tasted like ash on her tongue. "But I'll be back."

"I'm sure you will." A hint of a smile, revealing teeth yellowed by tea leaves. "And I'll receive you with pleasure."

She'd have the place searched, from corner to corner. Tear everything apart. But somehow she knew she wouldn't find the implants, that he was clever enough to have hidden them well. And that what she truly needed was a way to outwit him. She, the uneducated daughter, who had perfunctorily listened to her tutors' lessons and failed her examinations; who had little knowledge beyond a smattering of poetry, and etiquette...

She looked at the students again, at their bright, almost fevered eyes, their faces taut with the desire to learn; at the cut of their clothes, too trim and too neat, too eager to reflect wealth and ease. And she felt a long way from home again, as if she were back on the ship that had first brought her to Prosper, struggling to find herself amidst the strangeness of the deep planes, bereft of everything, as if she were already an orphan.

Linh stood in the banquet hall, watching the light shift from a warm red to the cold, heartless light of Old Earth's moon: a disk that slowly coalesced in the air above her, growing larger and larger until she could see every crater, every pockmark; even boyish, mythical Cuoi, sitting in the crown of leaves of his banyan tree. A fiction that had nothing to do with the Red Turtle star they orbited around, or with life as it was now, away from the husk of Old Earth.

The light played on the red pillars and the inscriptions

they bore, stretched out what was only a modest, low-ceilinged room into a place that could almost have belonged to a planet-side mansion.

Around Linh, the tables were spread: plates of silver, of nano-grown fibers made to look like the vanished celadon of old, and the fragile cups, the treasures of the family, all laid out for the admiration of Lady Oanh. It all seemed... pregnant with waiting, like the ancestral altar on the day of the bride's homecoming.

She'd have laughed if she hadn't felt so dead inside. If she hadn't been seeing, over and over, Giap's face hovering into her field of view; his mouth moving, reproving her for overworking herself yet again; his hands steadying her up, all but carrying her to the tribunal's kitchen where a steaming teapot would be waiting for her, and the familiar, nutty smell of the tea wafting up to her, a clear scent that flowed into her mouth.

She'd always insisted that Giap take a sip, but he'd smile and say she was the magistrate, and somehow she'd never managed to couch the request in such a way that he'd accept it...

Spirits, how she missed him.

The six voices within her were silent. Even First Ancestor Thanh Thuy had nothing to say, not even some clever quote about the duty of friends to one another.

Linh was alone in her own mind. She was thinking of the Xuyan Classics of Luu Bi, and the Oath in the Peach Garden; of friends not born together, but swearing to die together. And it frightened her. Giap would have told her that she was the magistrate, that she needed not grieve for the death of a subordinate, that parents did not weep for children as much as children for parents.

He would have told her all of this, and she would have known, in her heart of hearts, that he was right.

But she'd never listened to Giap, had she?

Xuan Rua slid by, bringing paper, an ink-stone and a brush onto one of the spare tables. "They'll be coming any moment."

"I know," Linh said.

Xuan Rua set a bowl of water by the side of the bowl, frowning. She looked at the ink stone again, and set it upright. Then, still looking away from Linh, she said, "Thank you for doing this."

Linh winced. She knew why she was doing this, and there was no good in it. "For Prosper," she said, thinking of Giap, of the message Quyen had hidden from her, of a place where nothing was private; everything was laid out like corpses on a morgue's slab. A madhouse ruled by the maddest one of all, far from the Way and its balance, far from Master Kong and his wisdom.

Giap, of course, would have urged her not to think about revenge. "For Prosper," Linh said again, and Xuan Rua's head tilted up, as if her student were about to break the rules of propriety in order to meet Linh's gaze, to look into its depths.

The gates to the room opened, and Lady Oanh walked in.

She looked much more regal than in Linh's quarters:

her áo dài tunic was of brushed, luminescent silk, its patterns slowly rotating, and their contours subtly altering as Lady Oanh crossed the length of the hall. The silk swirled around her like leaves lifted up by the wind. Her face was whitened with ceruse, her hair piled into an elaborate bun, eyebrows plucked into the shape of a moth's wings.

She looked like a queen from ancient days, truly a Lady from the First Planet, walking in the palaces of the Emperor himself, effortlessly consorting with the highest officials and the favoured concubines.

Behind her was a procession that seemed to include the entirety of Prosper: Cousin Quyen, of course, in green-hued robes embroidered with bamboos and pines; Bao and Huu Hieu, looking stiff and not at all pleased to be there; Cousin Kim-Ly, leading the younger children; and the other, more distant cousins from the rest of the family and a flood of other citizens Linh had never seen, a sea of coloured five-part dresses and long áo dài dresses, and resplendent jewellery that made her eyes ache.

Fake, all of it. A dance on the edge of the abyss in a station depleted by war. Fake, all of it, the smiles, the makeup, the averted gazes and the muttered polite nothings; the moon overhead, the ceiling that she knew was much lower, that was crushing her under its weight.

Fake.

The jostle for the tables had finished, leaving Linh in a spreading circle of silence. Lady Oanh was at the place of honour, with Quyen faced her, closest to the doors and the attendants with their waiting trays. Quyen was impeccably dressed. Of course, that was all she knew how to do, didn't she. Her face, as she raised it towards the guest, settled in the old, familiar, unbearable arrogance.

"I beg leave to say a few words, as we are gathered here," she said. "The times are not happy." Her face twisted in a perfect mockery of sorrow that she did not feel an ounce of. "But then, we of Dai Viet have spent so much time with war it might as well be an old friend. We have known the packing away of bamboo mats, and the flight into darkness; the lords of Trinh and Nguyen tearing Dai Viet apart, as we are torn apart now."

The past, offered up to explain the present, all so casually, so unfeelingly Linh felt her hands clenched. What about the dead? Would they feel comforted by knowing they were part of an endless cycle, a history endlessly closing in a circle; to know that, even among the stars, death and war and famine still stalked?

"But we are more than that," Quyen was saying. "We make the red candles burn high." She gestured, and the hall filled itself with red light, even as the moon seemed to shift and recede into the background.

"We serve the warm wine, and remember our friends scattered like wild geese; and we honour our guests tonight." Quyen dipped her head towards Lady Oanh, who inclined her own in return. It was an easy gesture, like the Emperor to a supplicant.

Platitudes, Linh thought, rubbing the ink stick against the wet stone and the glaze of black spread to her fingers, dark and sticky like unhealed wounds. Quyen might look smug, but she did nothing more than quote from a few half-remembered poems and stumble, blind, through a room full of the world's riches, snatching and mangling and calling it her own with misplaced pride.

"Lady Oanh, we are a miserly station on the edge of nowhere. We have no bright painters, no talented speakers of odes. But Cousin Linh has agreed to compose a poem for us tonight, in honour of this happy reunion."

And she looked at Linh, triumphant and smug, so sure of herself. She hadn't even thanked Linh for doing this; it had taken Xuan Rua to voice that particular thought. She was so secure in her arrogance, thinking she knew everything in the Heavens and on Earth, that she could command each and every one of them...Had she been so sure of herself, when she'd denied Linh the knowledge of Giap's death?

You don't own us, Linh thought, dipping the brush into the ink. Fifth Ancestor Hoang rose in her mind, whispering words about the beauty of the moon, meeting goddesses in the midst of clouds and rain, excursions to lakes on planets long dead. But no, that wasn't what she wanted. A banquet; an occasion for a reunion.

And for an accounting, too; something that would damage Quyen beyond repair.

For Prosper, Linh thought, tasting ashes and mud on her tongue. Behind Quyen, relegated to one of the lesser tables, was Huu Hieu, his face pale, ill at ease in the presence of so many people.

There is someone else...I'm leaving.

He was going away. Away from Quyen and her machinations, away from the stifling tomb that was Prosper. Up until this moment, Linh had not realised quite how much she envied him his freedom. You don't own us, she thought, to Quyen who couldn't hear her. You don't own him, and I'm proud that he can escape your clutches.

Taking her brush, she painted the verses on the paper in swift movements. The words tumbled atop one another in her mind, flowed like the waters of a stream, like the notes of a song. And every allusion was as clear, as pitiless as the sun on the steppes, as the sea in the morning after a storm, washing up corpses on the beach.

When she was done she stepped away, to look at the words. Xuan Rua was still standing by her side, her eyes widening as she read the poem. And Quyen…Quyen—*Underworld demons take her!*—was standing, smiling at her, waiting.

Linh spoke up without looking at the paper. The first couplet was a classic, speaking of the joys of friends meeting again:

> *The broken willow-twig is whole again, and the wild geese have flown homewards*
> *Fresh cooked rice with millet, and warm wine in the golden cups.*

But the answering couplet…

> *Caged birds flutter close, their wings drifting in the flame of the red candles*

A pair of most filial magpies, their fill eaten, kiss each other like lovers, and fly to Longevity.

Linh could see Lady Oanh frowning. The poem was barely short of suitable, the allusions of its last couplet casting a sinister veil on everything within the hall—the burning of the birds' wings, the image of hunger and cages…

And then, as the room fell silent, she realised what she had done.

Magpies. The symbol of love and marriages. The birds that went between the Herder and the Celestial Weaver, allowing them to meet and celebrate their love on the bridge of birds. Filial magpies. Huu Hieu's name meant "most filial"; and, as to the very last words…Longevity. Longevity Station.

She had…She had written the poem in a trance, meaning to damage Quyen's tainted hospitality. But, instead, she had besmirched Huu Hieu, revealed to the entire hall the existence of his lover, and his intention of leaving the station for Felicity. She had…

Spirits, what had she done?

A slow look of horror was stealing across Xuan Rua's face, leeching it to the colour of a shroud. Quyen's whole body had tensed; she was mouthing "filial" under her mouth. Her gaze, narrowing, travelled down the length of the banquet tables, as if struggling to find a face that would bring it all into focus. Lady Oanh's mouth opened, her arm tensed, opened in a gesture towards Quyen, as if she could stop Quyen from moving altogether.

Linh had been so proud of herself, so idiotically lost in the ecstasy of composing. But no, she couldn't excuse it that way; she'd meant it all, every spiteful word, even the denunciation of Huu Hieu, who had everything she couldn't have: a loved one, and a future away from Prosper Station. She'd meant it all, and she'd gone too far.

Quyen's gaze, narrowing, fixed unerringly on Huu Hieu. Then, too late, Quyen realised what she'd given away, as the first whispers started among the guests, the first spiteful words, the start of rumours that wouldn't die. Lady Oanh's hand had fallen back, and she had her mask on again, the magistrate on her dais.

Linh struggled to compose herself, but all she could see was Xuan Rua's eyes, like two holes into the torture pits of the underworld, and Huu Hieu's face, slowly decomposing as he realised the attention of the entire banquet hall was moving towards him. All she could see was the moon, shifting into fractured opalescence, its light slowly turning as black as tar, as the Honoured Ancestress' wail filled the room to bursting.

Quyen stood outside the heartroom, watching the light play on the station's walls. For the first time in her life she felt as if she were floating loose, as if she could see past the oily metal and the carefully constructed calligraphy, straight into the heart of space. And the heart of space was the void, a comforting refuge, a realm where nothing began and nothing ended, removed from the turmoil of the world.

From inside came fragments of words. This, like the

moon fracturing in the banquet hall, squeezed her heart into a thousand ice shards. The Honoured Ancestress had always kept an iron hand on Prosper Station's environment, and to see it drift out of control…

She kept herself standing straight, looking like the axle that linked the Heavens to the planets, even though she couldn't keep her own thoughts in order.

Over and over, she saw Huu Hieu's face, as the lights of the red candles flickered in and out of existence; felt the pressure in her ears waver and fall away as the Honoured Ancestress fell in and out of focus, Her comforting embrace sheared away from them all. She heard Cousin Linh's verses, biting into her mind like the fangs of a snake.

How dare she! How dare she accept Prosper's hospitality, and give them…*this* in return.

Xuan Rua was approaching, followed by her sister. Xuan Kiem's face looked as pale as polished metal, her hands shaking.

Rua, Kiem. Turtle, Sword; and there had been a baby girl who had died: Xuan Ho. Lake. A blatant reference to Emperor Lê Loi and his magical sword, who had wrested Dai Viet from China's grasp in the distant past. An unsubtle, almost vulgar use of the language. Emblematic, as in everything, of Huu Hieu's failures.

Xuan Rua bowed, briefly, as she neared Quyen. "Aunt."

"Nieces." Quyen kept her gaze away from the heart-room. It did her no good to endlessly wonder what Lady Oanh was going, or why she'd acceded to Quyen's request despite the utter disaster of the banquet.

Xuan Rua swallowed. Her gaze, uncontrolled, rising to meet Quyen's. "He had plans. Three berths on a merchant ship."

In those days of war berths on ships did not come cheap, no matter if they were mindships cutting through deep spaces, or the slower mainliners. "And that was why he needed to sell the implants."

It was not a question, and Xuan Rua did not treat it as such. "The mindship was *Baoyu's Red Fan*, but it left three hours ago, rather precipitously."

Of course. The news of the banquet had been around the station ten thousand times by now, and the captain had known enough to smell which way the wind was blowing. "And Lê Thu Anh?" Quyen asked. "The schoolteacher?"

"He wasn't on the manifest," Xuan Rua said. "But from what you were saying…I don't think he'd have left."

No. He would remain, burning with the desire to change Prosper, to give his students a chance to change the system. As if that would ever happen. There would always be the privileged; and if those weren't determined by blood, they'd be determined by talent and by intelligence. And how much fairer was that, for those to whom their ancestors had not bequeathed intelligence at birth?

She'd wasted time, trying to negotiate with Lê Tu Anh, to be conciliatory. No longer. Du Khach's implant was still on the station, or the Honoured Ancestress would have let her know. There was still hope that she could redeem herself, if she stopped being overwhelmed by events.

"Send Bao and the attendants to the Abode of Brush

Saplings, and search the place. Leave no stone unturned, no nook unexamined."

Xuan Rua nodded, but her face was pale. Poor girl, Quyen thought. It was bad enough to have responsibility thrust early upon her, but to have to deal with her father's failings, without a mother to support her…

"I'm sorry." Quyen thought back to what Xuan Rua had said. Three berths. It was obvious they were for him and his two daughters. "You didn't know?" Quyen asked Xuan Rua, though she didn't need to. Xuan Rua's face and Xuan Kiem's pallor made it all too clear.

"No," Xuan Rua said.

Xuan Kiem blanched as if struck, but she said nothing. Her usual arrogance and eagerness had been washed away by a flood.

"No," Xuan Rua said. "What did he want to do, Aunt? Did he" —she swallowed— "did he plan to drag us to the ship, without asking for our opinion?"

Quyen took a deep breath and said, slowly, "He's free to take you wherever he wants, nieces," she went on, before either of them could speak, "you're not of age, and he is not beholden to ask for your opinion before leaving." It galled her that the laws could be this misguided, but she could do nothing about that. "The law says there is nothing wrong with that."

"But…" Xuan Rua said, her face so pale it looked powdered with ceruse.

"That doesn't mean I approve of it," Quyen said, sharply. "And that doesn't mean he's free to do any of the other things: to sell our family implants like pitaya fruit at the marketplace, or to plan to run away from Prosper without asking leave of me or the Honoured Ancestress."

"He should have told us," Xuan Rua said.

Xuan Kiem's gaze was hard. "He was afraid we would refuse. He didn't trust us, did he?"

Quyen was saved from answering the awkward question when the door to the heartroom opened, letting Lady Oanh through.

She walked a little unsteadily, her poise a fraction from perfect, her legs shaking, almost beyond the threshold of perception. But all of Quyen's senses were sharpened. She would not be caught unawares again.

"Lady Oanh." Quyen and the girls bowed to her. Lady Oanh waved a dismissive hand.

"No need for that, between family." She pulled herself straighter, and the weariness disappeared. Something like a mask seemed to descend over her features, freezing them in the distant one of the statues in the temples. "You want to know about your Mind."

Quyen nodded, not trusting her tongue. She'd asked for that, schemed and bullied her way to this moment. But now that it was there, hovering over her like the executioner's silken garrotte, a hollow had opened in her stomach, a maw that seemed to leech all warmth from her muscles.

"Pham Lê Thi Mot," Lady Oanh said, slowly. "Conceived by Pham Van Vu, borne by Lê Thi Phuoc in her womb. Awakened for five generations." Her gaze was distant, as if she were already composing an official report. "I have conducted a thorough examination, given what was allotted to me, and I see no flaw of design. The five humours are properly anchored within the heart room, and the station itself was well prepared to welcome its Mind, everything in proper balance."

She fell silent. "But?" Quyen said, slowly. The word seemed to come from a faraway place, as if it had never belonged to her.

Lady Oanh's face moved a fraction, settling into another mysterious, unreadable expression. "Something has gone wrong. The khi flow has stagnated within the outer rings, and the elements are slowly freezing in place. She's losing her integrity, little by little."

The hollow in Quyen's stomach opened wide, chilling the marrow of her bones.

Silence followed. Then Xuan Rua said, "Forgive my audacity, but there has to be something we can do."

"Some…redesigning of key points on the station," Lady Oanh said, "would solve the problem. But it will also remove her short-term memory."

"Short-term?" Quyen asked.

"For the last generation."

Meaning, effectively, that the Honoured Ancestress wouldn't recognise them. That they'd excise a part of Her life, and expect Her to go on as before.

"It would take time," Lady Oanh said. "And skills."

"And a Master of Grand Design Harmony." Quyen couldn't keep the taste of ashes from her mouth.

"Not necessarily." Lady Oanh looked thoughtful. "As descendants of the Honoured Ancestress, you have access to the higher levels of the trance. This should be enough to make the adjustments you need. I will leave schematics with you, if you wish. But it has to be done...*precisely.* There can be no room for mistakes, or you'll lose more than short-term memory." She spread her hands. "You have a choice, though: it need not be done now. You can ask for a Master of Grand Design Harmony from the First Planet, and not take such a great risk."

"You said she was losing integrity," Quyen said, and she wasn't sure how to make it sound less like an accusation.

"Yes, she is deteriorating fast. But it'll stop, soon, once it has spread to all the non-vital functions. I think the obstruction dates back a generation or more; a series of mis-steps in the design. A series of...oversights on top of an old design. They didn't build Minds to be very robust, back then." She smiled, though she did not seem amused. "We all find it hard to project our imaginations beyond our own existence, and even less into the time of our great-great-great grandchildren. You can survive until a Master of Grand Design Harmony arrives. There are, after all, fail-safes to prevent her from depressurising the corridors, or flooding entire levels. You'll be cramped, but fine."

Cramped. Surviving; barely. "A decision," Quyen said. A slow decline or a loss. She wasn't sure whether to laugh or to weep. "Thank you," she said, slowly, carefully.

Lady Oanh shrugged. "It was the least I could do,

under the circumstances." She moved away, her gaze turned towards her spaceship, her own departure, and flight back to the capital. She'd gone no more than a few paces, slowing down with each of them, as if mulling on something, when she turned back towards Quyen. "Lady Quyen."

Whatever Quyen had expected, it wasn't this form of address, putting her on an equal footing with Lady Oanh. "I'm not a Lady."

"Nonsense." Lady Oanh's voice was brisk, business-like: she'd decided on her course of action, and nothing was going to stop her. "You might not administer a district tribunal, or a planet, but no one here will deny that you run Prosper. I have no idea why you persist in belittling yourself." She went on, before Quyen could splutter an appropriate response. "As magistrate to administrator, I'll give you a warning."

"I don't understand," Quyen said.

Lady Oanh's face was distant, once again. "I think you have enough to worry about without adding that. Expect one more ship to come to Prosper, quite soon."

A ship? A merchant ship? But no, why warn them about a merchant ship? It made no sense...

The smile that spread across Lady Oanh's face was halfway between sad and malicious. "Embroidered Guard."

Quyen had thought she couldn't grow any colder, any emptier. She'd been wrong. The Embroidered Guard, the Great Virtue Emperor's elite troops, only sent to reassert the Empire's power in the bloodiest way possible. "We have transgressed no laws," she started, and then the obvious answer hit her between the eyes like a barbed spike.

Cousin Linh.

Book 3
The Embroidered Guard

In the hours that followed the banquet, Linh became even more of a pariah than usual. The family provided for her, and her access privileges to the higher levels of the trance weren't cut off, but everything was given with tight lips, and her usual accesses into the Honoured Ancestress' and Quyen's chambers denied. Not that Linh had ever cared much about it, but she hadn't expected the whole situation to leave her...wrung out, empty, as if there'd been nothing left within her once she'd poured her bile.

Nothing but grief, and the emptiness where Giap had once been; the bitter knowledge that all her prayers, all her entreaties to her ancestors would not bring him back, would not fill the hollow in her heart. The ancestors on her implants, too, were silent, though she could feel First Ancestor Thanh Thuy's disapproval like a slap on the hand. No doubt she was keeping all the others silent until Linh realised the gravity of what she'd done.

It had been clumsily done. But Linh wouldn't go back on it, or on how she felt about Prosper.

The only one she felt sorry for was Huu Hieu. She'd

gone several times to his quarters, mustering an apology that rang false even to her. But the guardians at the doors of his chambers made it all too clear this access, too, was denied to her. Accordingly, she was down to using the trance, looking into the guts of the system, wondering if there was a weakness she could exploit to send him a personal message that bitch Quyen wouldn't read.

And what was in the guts was...frightening. Everything was haphazardly cobbled up, seeming to answer little more than random impulses within the core. Linh was no Grand Master of Design Harmony, no Mover of Bots, but still, even she could see that it was all wrong and getting worse by the moment. Quyen was losing her grip on the station. Linh watched, amused, as Bao and a posse of servants tore the Abode of Brush Saplings apart, looking for the missing implants, while the teacher, Lê Anh Tu, watched them, mockingly.

In the end they had to leave. Linh had no doubt Bao would report his failure to Quyen.

Good. Let the bitch know chaos, too. Let her know loss.

But even those words seemed to ring hollow in her mind, faded against the memory of the entire hall turning to her in the wake of her poem.

She was still looking into the system—like a spaceship pilot fascinated by deep spaces a moment before the ship's protection failed them and they were torn apart—when a visitor was announced.

It was Bao and he looked...different; the ethereal cast

to his face subtly wrong, like ill-applied makeup, or a corrupted mask.

He didn't bother with even so much as a greeting. "I can't find my younger brother."

Linh laughed, not bothering to disguise the bitterness in that laugh. "And you think I'd know where he is?"

"You're a magistrate." Bao's tone was flat, reasonable, a monk's, a priest's.

Linh wished she could just throw him out of her quarters, and not wonder what hid beneath the facade he'd been so busy constructing.

"Even if you weren't the family member he spoke to most, you're the one who is used to tracking down people."

"You're mistaken," she said. "I don't track people down. My lieutenants do."

"Did." Bao hesitated. "I've seen the records, Cousin. For what it's worth, I'm sorry for what happened. Quyen meant well, but no one should ever find out bad news the way you did."

Linh sighed. If it were only Bao and his belated good-wishes, she'd have made her position clear. But she owed Huu Hieu for shattering his dreams. Still, if Huu Hieu had managed to escape who was she to deny him?

"I can't help you," she said. "At least he's free, and I'm the last one who should deny him this."

Bao surprised her by openly grimacing, and she saw the worry in his eyes, as raw as bleeding skin. "If he's left, if he's escaped, then I won't pursue him. But there's always the other option."

"You think like Cousin Quyen," Linh said, slowly, carefully. "You'll want him to face the wrath of the family, like everyone else."

"You misjudge me." Bao shook his head, but he did not appear angry. "I didn't say I approved, but I understand. We all retreat from grief in different ways, and I know this all too well. If my younger brother's path to healing is away from Prosper..." He spread his hands. "I won't be the one who shatters him. I can't."

And that, if nothing else, was truth, a raw admission of the centipedes that had been wearing grooves into the skin of his heart for far too long. She wondered how long he'd nursed his uncertainties, realised she didn't even know, that she'd never asked. Misjudged, indeed.

"I don't know him as well as you do," Linh said, finally.

Bao shook his head. "I ceased paying attention to my younger brother long ago. A mistake. Tell me, Cousin, what do you think he'd do, if he couldn't leave?"

If he couldn't leave...

A vague queasiness was growing in her stomach. She hadn't thought he'd attempt to leave, not so soon after being found out and pilloried for it. It would take a while before the wounds faded, before he could think reasonably once more. She'd expected him to lick his wounds, nursing his grievances like warm coals. Not to run away...

He'd felt trapped on Prosper, until, at last, the jaws of the trap had opened. Freedom had been within sight. And he'd been denied at the last moment, his confidence betrayed, his secrets in the open, like a raw, pulsing wound.

The smile that played on Bao's lips could almost have been ironic, if there hadn't been such anguish in his eyes. "You know," he said.

"Yes," Linh said. "If he can't escape Prosper by ship, he'll try another way." Anything, rather than remain trapped.

Anything.

Even death.

She'd expected her mind to freeze, to run in circles in a blind panic. But instead, it slowly froze in another way, every thought coalescing like the facets of a crystal: clear and bright, with everything mercilessly thrown into focus, as this were an investigation once more, with Giap at her side and the militia ready to act on any orders she might have.

Suicide. Either by poison, strangulation, or drowning. Any other way would mutilate him in death, and she didn't think Huu Hieu was so far gone as to go join his ancestors by defacing the body that had been his parents' gift.

It was amazing, how clear-headed she found herself, removed from everything that might have interfered, any emotional attachment.

Linh closed her eyes, and went into the highest level of the trance she could access. "Honoured Ancestress."

She could feel Her, the vastness of Her thoughts; the shudders that ran through her, wracking Her like coughing fits. "You're sick," Linh said, horrified.

"Don't worry, child. I'm not dying yet." The Honoured

Ancestress made that strange sound which Linh knew to be laughter. But it sounded weak, done for Linh's benefit more than out of genuine feelings. "And Lady Oanh is taking good care of me." She sounded sad.

Don't cry, Linh wanted to say. I'm sorry for bringing so much grief to you. But, even in the trance, the words wouldn't get past her lips.

"Bao once told me you tracked everyone on Prosper Station."

There was silence, as in the moment before the storm died. "Yes. But I don't know, child. It's...been hard, currently."

"Even to track family?" Linh asked. "Huu Hieu?"

The Honoured Ancestress did not answer. Linh went on, in the silence, "I can restrict search areas if necessary. Any places with large bodies of water. The park with the Reclaimed Sword Lake, the water vats...And any apothecary on Prosper Station." And places to hang himself, too; but she didn't think he was going to try that. Finding a beam and a rope was much more effort than any of the alternatives.

Still that same disquieting silence. Linh hadn't realised until now how much she'd grown accustomed to the Honoured Ancestress's pressure against her mind.

At last, the Honoured Ancestress said, "In the fish sauce vats area. I can't locate him more precisely. I apologise."

"Don't," Linh said, more forcefully than she'd intended to, because it cut deep to hear the Honoured Ancestress hesitate, or be unsure of Herself. "Please."

A dry chuckle that made Her sound almost as She had before. "Don't worry, child. I'll take care of myself."

Her presence faded, and Linh almost believed Her last words.

Almost.

"The fish sauce vats," she said, every syllable leaving a numbing imprint on her tongue, like swallowing ice cubes. "How well guarded are they?"

By his grimace, she knew that they weren't. Linh got up. "Come on. We don't have time to waste."

The lights were flickering as they ran through the corridors. Though everything else appeared normal, Linh wondered how far the rot had spread. Prosper had been built on fragile foundations, and now the tide was crashing in, everything collapsing, as if the war and its disastrous consequences had followed her all the way to Prosper, like a messenger ahead of a defeat, carrying ill-luck into every house.

Steel and the glint of lamps; holos of paintings that twisted, rain pelting lonely mountains, waterfalls crashing into lakes, fishermen pulling net against the vast landscape of a river; and more modern paintings, passersby in the streets of a city decked in red lanterns; airships crossing each other between dizzyingly high buildings.

Corridor after corridor, each with their own ambience, their own muted music or poetry, and fragments of words following her; and Fifth Ancestor Hoang pressing against her mind until Linh could taste his fascination, his desire to speak, even against First Ancestor Thanh Thuy's prohibition...

Onwards, and every corridor seemed to merge into the next, until she was utterly lost. She called up the trance, felt it flicker against her mind, a weak overlay showing her the path to the starboard side of the station, where the fish sauce vats sucked in the light from the Red Turtle Star.

They couldn't be on time. It would take two, three minutes for a human being to drown? Perhaps more to be utterly past recovery by medbots; but still, Huu Hieu had had far more time than this. But he might not have had their desperate clarity, the need that even now turned Bao's face a muddy white that gripped Linh's heart with a fear she'd thought forgotten in the aftermath of Giap's death.

At last, at long last, they reached the widest room Linh had seen on Prosper: the curvature of its ribbed ceiling evident, its steel rafters unadorned. Light streamed in, curiously muted and reddish, coming from the tinted glass bay that occupied the back of the room. And over them towered the vats, the huge cylinders in which the small rice fish and the salt gradually macerated into pure, undiluted fish sauce.

They'd been wood in Ancient Dai Viet, but now everything had become metal, its components carefully assessed and assembled to ensure the best spread of flavour; and bots within the vats, their sensors wide open in order to make sure the fermentation was going as foreseen.

Bao's gaze was moving right and left, desperately trying to find something in the morass of readings. Linh called up the trance again but was blocked. It seemed the production of fish sauce was a secret kept on Prosper, even down to details on the contents of the vats. Her gaze, instead, roamed the alignment of vats, looking for any detail that didn't fit.

"There are hundreds of them," Bao said, his voice brimming with panic.

Linh raised a hand, cutting him off. Hundreds. But Huu Hieu was a man in a hurry, wasn't he? He wouldn't want the first vats, so close to the door: too obvious. But neither would he look for something too far away. Second row...

She moved, almost without thinking, towards the back of the room, her gaze tracking the vats. Nothing but the growing silence here, not ambient music or poetry to disturb the maceration, everything oddly deserted...

There.

A flash of a deeper colour in her sharpened vision and, as she moved closer, her pace quickened with each step. She saw the ladder leading to the top of the vat, which hadn't been retracted all the way. She reached out a hand. For a slow, agonising moment, she thought the station would deny her, but the ladder came sliding down as silently as a knife stroke. She clambered up its steps, heedless of whether Bao was following at all.

The sauce within the vats was a deep black, the same colour as the space between the stars, with an oily sheen that reminded Linh of the Honoured Ancestress' presence. And, in the midst of the blackness, a stain of something clearer: a tunic, a body floating face down.

Too late. Too late!

Footsteps behind her: Bao, clearing the top of the ladder. His eyes were blinking fast, not looking at anything beyond the trance. The surface of the liquid heaved up, bringing up a strong smell of ripe fish, and as the monitoring bots rose from the bottom of the vat, dozens of sleek metal crafts settled under the body, pushing it towards the edge; flipping it over, so that Huu Hieu's pale face stared up at them, his eyes glazed over by the black, thick liquid.

The odour of fermented fish was overpowering, bringing back childhood memories of watching Mother open up a bottle as Linh crushed garlic in a mortar and pestle: mixing the dipping sauces by hands as their ancestors had done for centuries instead of relying on the automatic kitchen, a pleasant memory turned sour by the proximity of death.

Bao knelt, pulled up Huu Hieu as if he were a sack of rice. Linh had no idea what he was doing, but his gaze had the familiar distant look of one within the trance. When he spoke, it was clear he wasn't relying on his eyes alone. "He's alive. Though he'll probably regret it, come morning. Come, give me a hand. We need to take him back to his quarters."

And Linh wasn't sure, after all, if she was going to weep or rejoice.

There was a ship.

It had emerged from the deep spaces, flaring into existence like the heart of a star even as Lady Oanh's own ship vanished, swallowed by the maw that marked the first step in her journey home to the capital. Its re-entry point had been a few days from Prosper; and now it hung in space, making its slow way to them, like the inexorable course of justice.

The Embroidered Guard, after all, never chose to hurry if they could avoid it.

The ship was sleek and deadly, like the blade of a knife, everything about it a weapon, from the sharp, angular protrusions on its hull to the cold sense of purpose that emanated from its Mind.

It had sent no comms, no call on the trance, but its destination was unmistakable. And so was its purpose.

Quyen had gone online, from the trance into the wider world, and looked at the edicts from the Grand Secretariat. She wasn't on the First Planet and couldn't easily search through them, so she read them one by one, until she found the name of Lê Thi Linh, Magistrate of the Province of Great Light for the Twenty-Third Planet, until she found the order that had made Cousin Linh a criminal.

Among all the offences within the Empire of Dai Viet, some were graver than others. Some called for punishment, not only on the offender, but on their kin.

Uttering treasonous words against the Dragon Throne was one of these, and the edict had made it all too clear that the Great Virtue Emperor had taken Linh's memorial as such. And, if she would not have the decency to ingest meds, or hang or drown herself, why, then, the Emperor would be all too glad to send guards to make his point.

Linh, and her kin. Of course, Dai Viet was merciful

and considered kin, not only through ties of blood, but through actions. A man's kin stood with him: wrote messages, shared death birthdays, births and funerals, and New Year's Eves. Or helped them, should they come as destitute refugees to a space station.

To the Embroidered Guard, all of Prosper would be kin, to the ninth generation, enough to encompass most of the inner rings of the station. All of them guilty of the same crime, and brought back to the First Planet for judgment and punishment—if the Embroidered Guard didn't decide to forgo procedure and summarily execute them all on the spot.

Better, perhaps, for the Honoured Ancestress to forget them all. Better that She not wake up, and wonder what had happened to Her descendants, what calamity could have erased them all from within the station. Yes, better than realising they'd been betrayed by their own openness, their own casual grant of hospitality to one who had never deserved it. Kin stood by kin, but Linh had taken that rule and callously broken it into ten thousand unrecognisable shards.

With a coldness she hadn't thought was possible, her heart as coiled as a rattan roll within her chest, Quyen went to see Linh.

Linh made her wait. Quyen stood in the ornate courtyard for a while, breathing in the smell of water from the fountain. It was unfair, almost, that here everything seemed normal, without a hint of the centipede gnawing at the Honoured Ancestress' insides.

When Linh emerged, she wore a shift of clear linen, more suitable for the privacy of one's quarters than for receiving visitors. The lights overhead had dimmed, recalling the fall of twilight. A deliberate insult, Quyen thought, but then she saw the drawn lines of the face, the red-rimmed eyes, and the slight, very slight quiver in the muscles, a loss of control grievous by an official's standards.

"What do you want, Cousin? I don't have time for any of this." Quyen flinched at the crudeness. Fine, if this were a time to let the masks fall, to behave like uncouth Barbarians, she could play this game, too. "You'd better find it, Cousin. Did you honestly think I would never find out?"

"Find what out?" Linh shook her head. "Look, I apologise, but—"

"It's going to take more than an apology." All the facts were there, one following the other like a perfect chain of thought, and all Quyen had to do was speak fast enough not to be interrupted. "You came here as a war refugee. You said the invaders had destroyed your tribunal, that you had nowhere else to go, and therefore had gone to seek refuge with your kin. With *us*. With Prosper. You took our hospitality, ate our rice and our fish sauce. You smiled at us—no, I won't say smile, because from the start you acted as if you were above us all, as if everything we did was of lesser value—and you thought I would never check what had sent you fleeing from the Twenty-Third Planet. I *know*."

Linh pulled herself up. Her face was pale, leeched of colours in the courtyard's dim light, like a ghost, risen from its tomb, the light accentuating the rough folds of her clothes until they seemed mourning garb. "You're the one who doesn't know anything, Cousin."

"You made that clear enough." Quyen hadn't meant the words, but they came up, spit like white-hot stones. "Did you really think me too foolish to understand a poem?"

"You're too foolish to understand anything."

"I understand courtesy, at least."

"Courtesy?" Linh spat the word. "You could have asked, couldn't you? Asked where I'd come from, or why? But no. You granted me an audience like an Empress, let the Honoured Ancestress question me, and then you sent me on my way and never worried about me anymore."

How dare she! How could she stand there, with everything that Prosper was in tatters, and look obscenely proud of everything she'd done? "You weren't content with overturning the harmony of this family, were you?" Quyen kept her voice flat, but it cost her.

"I think you did that on your own." Linh smiled, an expression utterly leeched of joy. "Ask your brother-in-law what he thinks of your family harmony."

"I won't waste tears on Huu Hieu. He's done enough for this station, don't you think?"

"Oh, I have no doubts." Linh's lips thinned, revealing teeth as sharp as fangs. "Including going off and attempting to commit suicide. But of course you only care because of the scandal, don't you? Better that he be dead than besmirch the family name. Better that his ghost linger over the fish sauce vats, while you bat your eyelashes and pretend to grieve, thinking that it's really all for the best, that a drowning is cleaner than a scandal."

Fish sauce vats? Drowning? "He wouldn't." Quyen's voice was flat. He'd always been a coward, always been inclined to retreat from the world, from his responsibilities. But this?

"I think his sense of family duty doesn't go that far."

Cousin Linh's smile was wild, feral. "Unlike yours, of course."

"And you're such a dutiful woman." Daring to stand there, Quyen thought, to make glib remarks about it all, flinging it into her face as if it were her fault. But...but Linh's face was drawn and taut, and the vague, familiar smell in the air was indeed that of fish sauce, not easily scrubbed from clothes and skin without proper bot instructions.

At least Huu Hieu had someone to care for him. The thought was low and savage in her mind, like a knife stroke. "As far as I'm concerned," Quyen said, slowly, "you two deserve each other. So go ahead and save each other's lives, or commit suicide. It won't make a difference now." Her hands had clenched into fists. "Not after you've brought the Embroidered Guard here to kill us all."

She hadn't thought Linh's face could get any paler. "What do you mean?"

But Quyen was no longer in the mood to trade insults. "Check the logs, Cousin. I'm sure you can work it out on your own. You're smart, after all; and I'm just a provincial housewife."

And she left, without turning back.

A knock at the door made Quyen look up. It was Xuan Rua and her uncle Bao. Xuan Rua was carrying rolled-up papers, an odd sight on a station in which barely anything was printed anymore. But then everything was falling apart, and the trance was no longer as accessible as it had been.

"May we come in, Aunt?"

Quyen nodded. She'd been trying to put the conversation with Linh out of her mind. She was unsuccessful, as every time she so much as blinked she'd see Linh's pale, arrogant face, accusing her of neglecting her own brother-in-law. The gall! The unbreakable, utterly unsuitable pride...

Xuan Rua's face was pale, her eyes rimmed with red. Bao's topknot was askew, with wisps of hair escaping from its confines, giving him the air of a dishevelled beggar. "You know about Huu Hieu?" Quyen asked.

Bao sighed. "Yes, but this isn't about him."

"I don't want to talk about Father's...achievements." Xuan Rua's face was harsh, as if she'd turned into her less naive sister overnight.

"I understand," Quyen said. "When more time has passed..."

"No. He has gone beyond the limit of what we can tolerate."

"You can't criticise your elders," Bao started, but Xuan Rua's gaze whipped towards him with the savagery of a leaping panther.

"Can't I? He's devastated this family and this station by thinking only of himself at every turn. I owe him filial piety; but it is also written that a child's duty is to show their father the way. Tell me I'm wrong."

"He's your father," Quyen said, wearily. "And part of the family. You won't ever change that." Much as they would all like to, they couldn't remove blood-ties.

Xuan Rua shook her head, and did not answer. "I came for this," she said, unrolling the papers she held on the low table. They were Lady Oanh's schematics, adorned in a cursive, effortlessly elegant script, and annotated here and there in Xuan Rua's crabbier handwriting.

"You've looked at them?" Quyen's cheeks burnt. She should have made time for this.

Xuan Rua made no remark. Of course she wouldn't; children didn't criticise their elders. "It's not complicated. All that it asks for are minor adjustments in the flow of the five elements in several places over the station. Most of those can be done in advance. Those, however, the very last ones…" Her hands rested, lightly, on Lady Oanh's beautiful, effortless calligraphy, pointing to the heart-room, and four places on the outer rings. "Those have to be done within seconds of each other."

In other words, coordinated through the trance, which was falling apart. "And if not done right?" Quyen was amazed at how steady her voice was.

"You know." Bao's voice was serene. "It's a risk."

A risk that she had to be willing to take, for the sake of Prosper, for the sake of the Honoured Ancestress. For a future none of them might see. And yet…She took a deep breath. "There are complications."

Bao looked mildly enquiring. Xuan Rua was bent on the schematics, and did not look up. "The Embroidered Guard is coming here."

Bao did not move, and Xuan Rua sucked in a sharp breath. "Why?"

It was the perfect opportunity to accuse Cousin Linh, to pour her anger and her bile. But she was weary of it all, of the strife, of the dancing on the edge of the abyss, weary of the family tearing itself apart. "It doesn't matter," Quyen said. "What matters is that there might be an extermination order for the lineage."

Bao was no scholar. It was Xuan Rua who looked up, and said, "How far does it spread?"

"I don't know. I'll do my utmost to ensure it doesn't extend to you." The younger generation, the children, the future, everything Prosper would and could become. It would not be wiped out.

"It's Cousin Linh, isn't it?" Bao said. "The act of welcoming her on Prosper made her kin to us."

Quyen leant back in her chair, feeling a great weariness descend upon her. Everything was bleak, and she saw no way out. "I'll lie. Say I was the only one involved in welcoming her."

"And you think they'll believe this?" Bao asked.

Perhaps. Perhaps not. "It's worth a try. They might be kind, or merciful." Quyen knew, though, in her heart of hearts, that they would be neither. "Tell me again about the adjustments," she said to Xuan Rua.

Her niece was pale, but her voice did not waver as she outlined her plans, from fixing the small things to coordinating the last stage of renewing the Honoured Ancestress. "You did well," Quyen said.

Xuan Rua flushed. She'd grown in maturity. What a pity that all of that had come at such a high cost.

Quyen sat back, pondering, and sought out the trance.

"I can't make the decision for you," she said.

For an awful, quivering moment, she thought that the Honoured Ancestress had not heard her. But then Her voice spoke in her ears, low and wan, like a sick woman's. "Neither can I, child."

"You're old and wise," Quyen said, and heard Her laugh.

"I am selfish, child, and scared. I would rather everything went on as it has always done. I would rather remain by your side, and be your guide."

"I can't. I just can't."

"You have made all the decisions before," the Honoured Ancestress pointed out, gently. "Why would this one be different?"

"I don't…" Quyen thought of Lady Oanh's words, and realised she was lying to herself. "I run the station, but this is different."

"No different."

"Yes. It is your life, Honoured Ancestress. I won't make your choices for you."

"As you did for Linh?"

"I did nothing to Linh that she did not choose for herself."

A low, soft chuckle. "Perhaps. Perhaps not. Forgive me, child. My mind is wandering. But you know there is only one choice I can make, that any of us can make."

"But…you'd leave us alone," she wanted to say. "You'd leave *me* alone." And then she remembered the bitter knowledge: children weren't beholden to their parents. "Lady Oanh said… that it could go on." That there were fail-safes, that she might hurt them, but that she wouldn't kill them.

"You wish me to sow chaos among you once more?" The Honoured Ancestress' voice was low, ironic. "This isn't what I was designed to do, child. The fail-safes will keep you alive; but there is more to life than merely living it."

Good fortune, children, long life, Quyen thought, before she could stop herself. And would the Honoured Ancestress not lose it all—the children that would become strangers, the memories of her life vanishing, and their good fortune wrecked by the Embroidered Guard?

"It might all be for nothing. With the Embroidered Guard upon us…" Quyen had never been a good liar, and she knew it.

"I can lie," the Honoured Ancestress said, low and serene.

"You're not human." She was a Mind, impervious to the passage of time, present in ten thousand places at once. But she followed rules and logics which had been set down by humans. "You weren't made to lie."

"Neither was I made to fall apart," the Honoured Ancestress said, gravely. "Or to malfunction. I can try, at the very least."

It wouldn't work, Quyen thought, but could not say it aloud, could not contradict an elder.

"You worry too much, child," the Honoured Ancestress said. "Take each thing as they come, within the flow of the universe."

The flow of the universe. She was the one who faced the darkness of oblivion, and She could still give lessons in humility. "Oh, Grandmother." Quyen stifled a bitter laugh, staring at the darkness. "What will we do without you?"

The Honoured Ancestress said nothing. The touch against Quyen's mind faded, and she found herself staring at Xuan Rua and at Bao. "She agrees." She kept her voice cool and steady, as if she were not breaking inside. "Go seek out the rest of the family. We might as well do this before the Embroidered Guard arrives."

Huu Hieu in repose looked, if anything, worse than he had in the vat. What the bots had pulled had looked like a corpse, and had allowed her the illusion of thinking him dead. What Linh saw now turned her stomach: the skin that looked too pale to be natural, the bruises on the throat and under the eyes a darkened blue, like ink that had lost its virtue; the shorn scalp, glistening with perfumed oil; and the faint smell of fish sauce that seemed to cling to him, no longer the bright memories of childhood, but the rank, sour odour of rotting fish.

The Embroidered Guard. They were coming.

It wasn't the arrest, or even the thought of being brought back to the capital as a prisoner. Linh's family had long since died, and she would not disappoint them, or even bring punishment upon them. She did not fear death, or shame, but rather it was the thought that her memorial had been for nothing, that her words would be dismissed as the ramblings of a diseased mind, and that the war would go on, tearing the Empire apart.

That people like her and Giap would have died for nothing, changing nothing in the world.

Then again, she was one to talk—the brilliant scholar, the fearsome magistrate without a tribunal, standing in a spirits-forsaken station and railing about the world. As if she'd ever made a difference. What arrogance!

Another, better scholar would have committed suicide. Linh had no such courage.

So, after all, she thought, looking down at Huu Hieu, perhaps I am the coward, and you the braver one of both of us. Perhaps. He would have laughed at the thought, had his lungs not been wrung out by bots to resuscitate him.

The room's wall were painted the red of good fortune, and the closed doors bore guardian spirits on both sides to keep evil spirits out, and to prevent the ghosts of the dead from flitting around Prosper. A strong smell of camphor and musk rose from Huu Hieu's body: ointments for the healing of wounds, for keeping the body warm against the cold of the underworld.

She was turning to leave the room, when something brushed her, a fluttering touch that was all too familiar. "Honoured Ancestress?"

"He is awake, child," the Honoured Ancestress said.

What? Linh's gaze moved to Huu Hieu. His eyes were closed. But no, they were blinking, and a thin, narrowed line trembled between the upper and lower eyelids. Awake. Watching. Too weak to speak, or too angry to do so.

"You are…" Linh said, but the pressure against her mind was weak, the thin liquid of blood leaking away from cut veins. "I'm sorry," she said, though she wasn't quite sure why.

"You worry too much, child. This is no longer your business. Leave the family to sort its own problems."

The family, which did not include her. Of course. It was only to be expected, after what she'd done "I don't worry," Linh said. But the Honoured Ancestress was gone, leaving an odd emptiness in Linh's stomach.

Huu Hieu was still watching her. He lay back like a corpse, with only the eyes alive in the whole of his face. But his voice, when he spoke, was perfectly composed. "They say you and Brother Bao pulled me from the vat."

"Yes." Linh found herself moving. Everything felt so far away, seemed to be happening to someone else on some distant planet. Her hand moved towards his and rested, lightly, on the bruised and pallid flesh. "I'm sorry." She called up the trance, felt its shards gathering itself around her, and felt the Honoured Ancestress's touch across her mind, light and fleeting, and infinitely more frightening than the pressure.

The landscape that took shape was ruined. The mountains Linh had called up reared against a torn sky, with stars falling like rain from the devastated Heavens. The grass under their feet was run through with cracks; beyond the island of safety where they both stood, the landscape dissolved away into darkness.

Huu Hieu, grimacing, stood tall. But even in the designed environment his skin was awfully pale, with the bluish marks of the bruises at his throat, shining in the starlight through the cracks in his robes. He watched her, as if waiting for something more, and she wasn't sure she could give him the words.

"I thought I could be smarter than Quyen. I never meant to..." Linh's words trailed into insignificance, swallowed by the darkness around them, by Huu Hieu's burning gaze. "But I won't apologise for pulling you from the vats."

Huu Hieu made a low, rasping sound. It was only after a while that she realised it was laughter, coming from lungs that remained weak, even in this environment. Everything about him seemed smaller than it had been and in a way she couldn't pinpoint, for he'd never been someone she respected, not like Giap or Lady Oanh.

"Oh, Cousin," he said. "That was the most graceless apology I've ever heard."

"And have you been hearing many of them, lately?"

That silenced him. She realised how sharp, how unpleasantly cutting she'd become. "I'm sorry." Linh brushed her hands against the silk of her robes, feeling the cloth under her fingers, fibre by broken fibre. "I only came to see how you were doing. But I don't want to disturb you further, and I'm the last person who should be here."

"You're the only one." Huu Hieu's gaze was mirthless.

"Hasn't your brother—"

"My brother's a coward." His eyes burnt with an expression that made her uncomfortable, even though it wasn't directed at her. "He spit out the world a long time ago, and he hasn't looked back."

"He saved your life."

"Perhaps," Huu Hieu said. "Or perhaps that was you."

Both of us. You wouldn't still be alive if it hadn't been for both of us. "The girls have been here, I'm sure." She wasn't sure where the perverse desire to contradict him came from; how she, of all people, found herself defending Prosper and its family. "You're not alone, Cousin."

"After this, I might as well be. Quyen will make sure that I'm never alone again, never trusted again. Spirits, I'll be lucky to be invited to the family banquets." Again, that rasping sound. "You showed her she wasn't mistress of Prosper. I'm glad for that, if nothing else."

"I...I did this to you." All of this: the empty room where

his body lay, the faint smell of fish sauce, the door that wouldn't open from the inside, the taut face that looked as though it would split open to reveal the cruel smile of a demon. She wanted to apologise again, but how many times could she repeat empty words without becoming empty herself?

Huu Hieu blinked, slowly. "We did many things to each other, cousin, and I don't think it will do us any good to keep track of it all. It's this place, this wretched place, where they never stop watching, where they never stop judging. It makes monsters out of us." His voice was shaking.

And some of us are already monsters, First Ancestor Thanh Thuy said in Linh's mind. Her disapproval spread like an ink stain, dirtying everything it touched. Linh extended a hand, touching Huu Hieu's skin, feeling it yield against her fingers, too soft and supple to be anything but that of an old man.

"Peace, then?"

"Peace." Huu Hieu smiled, bitterly. "We're both the same, after all. You and me against the world. Against Prosper, against Cousin Quyen."

Both the same. And welcome to each other, with Cousin Quyen's blessing. The thought rankled, somehow. Both the same. The eyes trained on her burnt with hatred, and that seemed to be the only thing left to Huu Hieu, the only emotion animating him: not love, not affection for his daughters, or belief in his own future. "You're going to try again, aren't you."

Huu Hieu said nothing. Behind him, the sky was falling apart. All the stars were gone, and the darkness deepened to reveal an abyss hungry for all human lives into which everything was falling, from Linh to the Honoured Ancestress to the whole of Prosper.

"I'm sorry," Linh said. "Of all people, I don't have the right to ask you this. You don't want me to know." But she knew, already. As Bao said, she'd taken his measure, and seen everything there was to see. He'd try, again and again, until he was finally successful. And he wouldn't be doing it to escape Prosper and a life grown too confining, or to keep the dignity he'd had in life.

No, he'd do it because he wanted to rankle Quyen. Because he wanted to show her that she wasn't mistress of his fate; and to leave her to deal with the scandal and the mess of his suicide.

She could have appealed to his love for his daughters, but she knew already that it had been scoured clean away from him, that he was a husk, a ghost already moved by anger, hungering only for revenge.

We are the same.

And the thought was a stain within her, spreading like First Ancestor Thanh Thuy's disapproval, like the Honoured Ancestress' touch. The same. Shambling corpses, exhaling only hatred, hollowed out by it. The same.

"No," she said, slowly. "You're right. I don't want to know." She let the environment fall away; stared down at him, old and hollowed before his time, and felt revulsion rise in her like a wave.

Slowly, she walked towards the door, emptied of everything, standing balanced upon the Great Void. She wanted the world to fold itself back and embrace her. She wanted Giap to be alive, her tribunal overflowing with complainants, and none of that would ever come to pass. Child. The Honoured Ancestress had named her well; had named them well.

Her fingers were digging into the skin of her palm, so hard blood flowed. Child. Named well.

At the door she turned, stared at Huu Hieu, until he looked puzzled. "Linh? What's the matter?"

"She was wrong." Linh's voice started low, and gained with every word; the magistrate's mask slipping on once again, lending her the strength she'd lacked since the beginning. "Wrong, don't you see? We're not the same, Cousin. And I'll prove it to her."

If Huu Hieu said anything behind her as she turned away, she didn't hear it. The door closed and cut her off from him. The metal of Prosper Station lay between them like an unbreakable wall, like a broken bridge across Heaven, one that could never be mended.

Quyen stood in the heartroom, watching a simple thing: a clock on the walls, wedged between the flowing lines of text. Another clock, a physical one, with a mechanism of shimmering metals that made a noise like a heartbeat, stood at the foot of the Honoured Ancestress' core, marking time.

Quyen held the trance, lightly. She felt the Honoured Ancestress's presence recede as Bao and the other members of the family moved eight-sided mirrors, drove copper nails, and cut through cables, rerouting the power to empty sections of corridors; shifting the balance of the elements within the station, smothering the Honoured Ancestress's voice.

The equivalent, she thought, shivering, of putting a man to sleep before opening up his brain. That was the schematics.

Around her, the station was deserted. They had notified the inhabitants of Prosper to remain inside their homes. As the power receded, the lights and the temperature regulation became more erratic, discouraging people from wandering outside.

Quyen held a single blade in her hand and watched the clock. When the time was right, she would cut the three cables in the centre, moments after Xuan Rua and the others cut three cables in their own section. This would reroute the power...

No, this was the wrong word. It would render the Honoured Ancestress unconscious, and, when She woke up again She would have to mould herself to Prosper's new shape. And She would be irretrievably, irremediably changed.

She could hear the breath of the Honoured Ancestress, coursing around her through every vent and every metal sheet, until the entire room seemed to be Her trembling body. She could imagine the station from the outer rings to the family quarters; she could breathe in, and remember that it would never, ever be the same again.

The colours around her were slowly bleeding, the pressure in the room rising to meet the hollow in her stomach. "Child." The Honoured Ancestress' voice was small, as if coming from very far away.

"Grandmother." Her throat felt dry and everything seemed to be far away from her, happening in another of the myriad worlds under the Buddha's gaze. "I'm sorry, we didn't find Du Khach's implant." Bao and the attendants had searched the school, thoroughly, and found nothing. "I would have liked you to have it." A last gift, to reassure the Honoured Ancestress, at the very end, to show Her that Quyen could keep her promises, that she was capable of guiding the station in the lonely years that would follow.

The pressure against her mind was kind, a mother's gentle caress. "It doesn't matter, child. You have other things to worry about."

But it did matter, in the light of all her other failures and of the decision sitting on her shoulders like a demon, gnawing away at her mind. "Grandmother, there is still time."

Silence. The pressure abating a fraction, like a stuttering heartbeat. "No," the Honoured Ancestress said. "I won't live like this, child. I cannot."

"I don't want to lose you," Quyen said, every word burning like a hot stone in her throat.

She remembered her first time in Prosper. She stood in a corridor, just on the other side of the wall from the ship that had brought her in, going to meet a husband she had only exchanged a few calls with—her own ancestors honoured by her sister's children, her family line merging with his own, everything that had made her until now undone, flapping loose in the wind like torn flesh.

She remembered the crushing loneliness, that same sense of standing on the edge of the abyss with no way but down, into a darkness deeper than that of the underworld, until the Honoured Ancestress had reached out, taken Quyen under Her protection. There had been a promise that she would never be alone until the day she died.

Broken now, all broken into ten thousand shards, like her five organs.

"It is the way of the world," the Honoured Ancestress said. "Oblivion and rebirth, and oblivion again." She sounded oddly wistful. Perhaps afraid? Quyen couldn't tell anymore. "As all humans do."

"But you're not human." Not immortal, but as close as, from their point of view. She'd seen them arrive, had seen children born, old men and women die, generation after generation. She...

The Honoured Ancestress' voice was soft. "I was built to watch over this station, for generation after generation. To watch over you all. How can I do my duty, if the madness is upon me?"

"You're afraid," Quyen said, and the Honoured Ancestress did not answer. Quyen realised that she was the one who was afraid, the one who would lose everything.

At last, a softer touch, almost like a hand stroking her

cheek. "I'm sorry, child. I truly am. But I will forget everything. Your arrival, and the years we spent together, and the banquet…"

"I'll remind you." Quyen's voice was low and fierce, with a fire she hadn't known she possessed. "Again and again." And she knew it would mean nothing to the Honoured Ancestress, that the Mind they had known, the *person* they had known, would be gone. That She would find their reminiscences baffling, like a blind man listening to a description of a painting they couldn't see, like an illiterate peasant in the old days, struggling to understand allusions from books they'd never read.

She knew that, once again, she'd stand in the vastness of Prosper and feel loneliness crushing the marrow of her bones, the entire station a strange and alien place that bore no resemblance to the home she'd made.

"You and Anh," she said, slowly. The Honoured Ancestress and her husband, the only two things she'd call hers in the entire world.

It wasn't fair. But then again, the world wasn't, was it?

The station was all but deserted, and the vapour of Linh's breath hung before her as she moved between the hologram stands. They were blinking out, one by one, and the lights were dimming, as if some huge hand were cutting off the power to all quarters.

Ring after ring, and everything was the same: the corridors empty, even more so, with the paintings gone, the music extinguished, and the clever poems faded away into nothingness. There was no noise but Linh's own footsteps, painfully echoing against the metal walls, with nothing and no one to muffle their echo. Tap, tap, tap, a noise coming back to haunt her, and her breath burning in her throat, as if she walked in the ruins of the war.

"Honoured Ancestress?" she asked, but got no answer. The trance, too, seemed to be weak and erratic. The only thing it displayed was a simple warning: "Stay inside. This is for the good of Prosper, and for our continued survival." Some reference to a poem, or a book, but Linh couldn't figure out which one. And so she walked in the gathering dark, feeling more naked and alone than she'd ever been.

Was it her doing? A poem. It had been nothing more than a poem. Surely it could not have collapsed Prosper upon itself?

Surely...

She'd seen all she needed to see. Before, she'd been locked up inside her quarters, and foraging through the remnants of the trance, trying to find a weakness, any weakness, that she could use against Cousin Quyen...

What irony, in the end, that she'd found another use for the information, that, instead of tearing the family apart as Huu Hieu had done, she would play her part in preserving its harmony.

The school was deserted when she arrived, its name blinking in washed-out letters over the entrance. Abode of Brush Saplings. Well named, for a place which trained scholars.

Linh's hand lingered on the control panel. She put her weight against the screen and pushed. With the station all but gone, and her status undetermined, it probably wouldn't work. She wouldn't be able to use her family's blood to bypass security.

The door swung open with a creak like the tortured souls of the underworld. Linh walked through, into an empty courtyard where the wind was rising, gathering whirls of dust. At the centre was a pond. The red carps inside had gone into a frenzy with the loss of light, sending splashes of water all over the central statue.

"We're closed," a peevish voice said, from behind the covered desks.

Linh smiled, and drew herself upright, effortlessly calling upon her magistrate's mask. "I think not. Will you deny me, Lê Anh Tu?" Instead of the address of "uncle", or "teacher", which she should have given him, she used his full name, as if he'd been called before her tribunal.

His voice was cold. "You're no magistrate, woman. You're a spirits-cursed refugee, even less than I am."

"Do you think so?" Linh's lips curled up.

"I know perfectly well who you are." Above them the ceiling was darkening, like night falling across a world that had never known it. "Mistress Quyen's poor, neglected cousin. A relation she'd deny if she could. Do you wish to regain her favours, after the scandal? It's too late." He shook his head, looking at the dust swirling all around them. "Much too late for anything. But we'll survive. Prosper will survive."

"You won't," Linh said. "Mistress Quyen will tear you to pieces if she doesn't find her implants."

Tu shrugged. "She won't dare. I told her already. She can search all she wants, and she won't find anything. She's sent her attendants already, and they've failed. Without proof, she can't touch me. There will still be a school, and I will still give my students the chance they deserve. And she can send all the relatives she wants, even the failed magistrates, but it will change nothing. Not one of you will find anything."

Magistrate. Bao had seen, after all, what made her so powerful, what made her such an asset to Prosper. Linh's eyes roamed the courtyard. Everything was empty, deserted, save for the central pond. "Do you know why they call us father-and-mother of the people, Lê Anh Tu?"

"Because you lord it over us all." He spat the words like poison snakes. "Because you're always right, no matter what we do."

Linh smiled. "Because we know people like parents know their children." Her hand rose, pointed towards the desk. "I've seen enough. I've heard enough. You're a bitter man, Lê Anh Tu, and an arrogant one. A smarter man would have moved the implants away, but you needed to feel their presence every day. You needed to remind yourself of the victory you'd won over the family."

"I don't care about the family!" Tu snapped, but there was fear in his eyes.

"They're here," Linh said, and she didn't need to look at him to see the confirmation. "In some place you think people won't touch, no matter how desperate." A handful of desks, under the roof, the ancestral shrine for Tu's own family, with an offering of fruit and the remnants of a stick of incense in a burner. The pond with the frenzied carps, and a door leading into the private quarters. The carps? No, too obvious. Most people would hesitate to gut a fish that stood for wealth. But it wasn't protection enough.

She moved, coming to stand before the ancestral shrine. "You can't..." Tu said, but she cut him by raising a hand.

"I think, too, that you're a man who cares little about the rules that keep us working, that you'll bend anything to the service of your cause." Had she still been a magistrate, she'd have kept a watch on him. From such fertile earth were murderers born, secure in their conviction that they could do no wrong as long as the cause was just, tearing away the fabric of society in the name of their so-called justice.

The wall before her was covered in rows of alcoves. In each was a small hologram stand, projecting the posthumous name of an ancestor and the distinctions they'd achieved in their lives: the ranks held as an official, the number of children, children and grandchildren; the battles they'd distinguished themselves in.

At the very top of the wall were distinctions dating back to Old Earth, and battles against kingdoms since long crumbled into dust. Everything seemed neat and ordered, with nothing out of place, strangely reassuring in a station gone mad. Though, of course, the holos would run on emergency power. Ancestors wouldn't be erased so easily.

She looked down at the fruit: a papaya, and a mango glistening in the dim light. Neither appeared to have been tampered with. Her gaze, rising, roamed the alcoves again, and caught on one that seemed slightly askew, its display slightly higher than the others, a minute disturbance that should have remained invisible. But Linh's sight had been modified in the Imperial Palace, giving her far greater accuracy than most ordinary men.

That one.

She could be wrong. She could be right. But either way she'd have a mob of howling ghosts after her, angered that she'd dare to disturb their shrine. "I, the magistrate of the Province of Great Light on the Twenty-Third Planet, humbly apologise for my presumption in disturbing you." And, before she could think on the enormity of what she was doing, reached out, and grasped the hologram stand, as Tu screamed beside her.

It came away in her hand, far heavier than it should have been. The bottom unscrewed, revealing a cache which contained three mem-implants smelling strongly of disinfectant.

She slid them in her sleeves, and smiled at Tu. "I think that's all the proof we need, don't you? *Child.*"

She left him in the darkened courtyard, turning the hologram stand over and over in his hands, his gaunt face twisted out of shape in anger, in grief. The air smelled of stale incense, and everything seemed to be collapsing around him. But, for him, she had no pity.

Outside night had come, stealing across Prosper like a knife across the throat. The lights that were never turned off were dark, and the walls were all blank, as empty as Linh's mind. The mem-implants weighed nothing in her hands: a breath, a word, a verse, nothing that should ever have the power to change the world.

Linh walked in the darkness, in the ruins. Gradually, her ancestors rose at her side: First Ancestor Thanh Thuy, tall and stern in the robes of President of the Metropolitan Court; Second Ancestor Huynh, smiling a crooked smile; Third Ancestor Vu, nonchalantly waving a fan, as if in the gestures of some secret language; Fourth Ancestor Canh in the white robes of mourning for his parents, Fifth Ancestor Hoang, her grandfather, his sleeves stained by ink; and Sixth Ancestor Hanh, Linh's mother, looking taller than she'd ever had in life.

And behind them were the shambles of her tribunal; the dead, lying in broken heaps; the streets overrun by the enemy's armies, and the screams of men and children and Giap, standing on the execution field with the executioner's garrotte around his neck. He was looking straight at her, his weathered face creased in a satisfied smile.

Her ancestors, too, were smiling at her; her mother extending a hand as if in blessing, and Fifth Ancestor Hoang was nodding at her. *Do what is right, child.*

And Linh said nothing, only walked forward, not feeling the rising wind.

* * *

"Mistress Quyen."

Quyen looked up from the package in her hands to see the face of a stranger. The entire family was still deep in the bowels of Prosper, making the last of Lady Oanh's adjustments. The Honoured Ancestress' presence had faded in her mind as time passed, until only a whisper remained, engraved in the flesh of her heart.

Remember me, child. And then, so faint it might as well have been a dream,*I am afraid...*

And then, the station has slowly started up again. Light had returned; the paintings on the walls had re-emerged as if they'd never been gone, though everything seemed subtly different.

The trance wasn't back yet, and her calls to the Honoured Ancestress had gone unanswered. Perhaps it was just as well. She was afraid of what would happen when that familiar touch would steal across her mind, and talk to her as if she were a stranger.

"Mistress Quyen." The boy waited, eyes lowered. He couldn't be more than thirteen years old, certainly too young to deliver messages.

"What is it?" she asked, more acerbically than she'd intended.

"There is a ship in the docking bays, Mistress Quyen." The boy swallowed, convulsively. "They say they won't be long, but..."

"What ship?" Quyen asked, although she already knew the answer.

"They say they're Embroidered Guard."

Quyen looked again at the package. Spread across the palm of her hand, as heavy as stone, were Huu Hieu's mem-implants. All three of them, neatly wrapped up, warm against her flesh, almost too warm to be held up for long.

There was a message, too, inscribed in a flowing style she recognised from her nightmares, the effortless curves of a trained scholar. She could see where the hand had shaken, when the ink had spilled. But it was all pristine nevertheless, suitable for displaying as an exemplary example of calligraphy that shone a light into the heart and soul of the writer:

There is nothing I can offer you that would be a suitable apology. Take, then, this small gift as a token. I hope you will, in time, bring yourself to think of me without hatred in your heart.

And a small, inscribed couplet, almost as an after-thought:

I have eaten the fresh cooked rice and the millet, and drunk the warm wine in the golden cups
And found it all tasted as bitter, like old stains upon lacquered wood
Let the wild goose fly away, much as it has arrived.

All of which was transparent enough. Even the poem which a child could have deciphered. Except that it made no sense.

"You were never very good at verses, were you?" Quyen said, aloud, and the boy, startled, looked up at her.

"Mistress?"

"Never mind," Quyen said. She laid the mem-implants in her chest, and took a last look at them before closing it. Their edges winked at her in the returned light, making the world waver and fold back upon itself. She thought of Du Khach, the ancestor in the implants, who had known the Honoured Ancestress such a long time ago, whom She might even recognise and cherish. She thought of Linh, and of the odd way the ties of blood pulled at each other.

"Get me to the docking bays. Quickly."

As they ran from the family's quarters to the docks, she felt it, rising in her bones: the fledging Mind, spreading from the core outwards, tentatively testing Her powers. Like a child, she thought, except that the Honoured Ancestress would remember more, wouldn't She? Lady Oanh had said She'd lose only a generation, but only if it were done right, precisely and painstakingly. And how did she know that what they'd done had been right at all?

I'm afraid, the Honoured Ancestress whispered, over and over in her memory.

She felt the pressure at the back of her mind, saw the oily stains, spreading across the paintings, cutting across the poems, felt the station buckle and strain, and still she ran. Alone.

At the docks she followed the signs to the doors of the only docked ship. It lay on the other side of Prosper's walls, with only a tube-door extending into the station, and she couldn't see it. But she could imagine it, only too well, sleek and sharp and deadly, tearing through the deep spaces as it made its way towards Prosper, towards its waiting quarry.

Towards them. She slowed, remembering that it wasn't only Linh at stake, but quite possibly the entire family, if orders had been given in that direction.

She walked the last turning in the corridor, as regal as any lady-scholar, as any court-spouse. She held her head high, hands relaxed at her side, in spite of the spreading cold, wrapping around her heart like a tightening fist.

There was a knot of people standing by the ship's tube-door, as if waiting for her. Burly Embroidered Guards surrounded a figure—Cousin Linh?—who faced away, towards the waiting ship.

Ahead of the group of guards, a single man stood, watching her approach with narrowed eyes. His skin was as dark as any Viet's, but the clear green eyes in the circle of his face attested to some mixed ancestry. He held himself straight, with the easy grace of those in power. Like all the Embroidered Guards, his body had been enhanced with metal, and the weapons grafted on his arms glinted in the harsh light of the corridor.

Quyen bowed, slowly, carefully, as if she were in the presence of the Emperor, which wasn't far away from the truth. The Embroidered Guard was the Emperor's will, and they bowed to no one else. "This station is honoured by your visit, my Lord."

The man grunted. "No need for politeness, Mistress. I presume you're Quyen, the Administrator."

Of course they'd be well informed. "Of course," she

said, slowly, forcing herself not to tremble, "if there is anything you need…"

She let the words hang in the air, like the silken thread of the executioner's garrotte. At length the man grunted again. "No need, Mistress. Your cousin has made things quite clear to us."

"I don't understand." Her gaze moved from Linh to the Embroidered Guard, and back to Linh again, who wouldn't meet her gaze.

"She said that she was here without your knowledge. That you gave her no shelter, and only recently discovered that she was there at all when she threw the entire station into an uproar." His gaze roamed upwards, into the weak lights, the shuddering walls, all the signs that the Honoured Ancestress wasn't there. "That you acted as no kin to her."

No kin to her!

That meant Prosper would be safe. The Embroidered Guard's eyes were still on her, lightly ironic. She could tell that he didn't believe a word of it. "You…" she said.

"I have heard what I have heard." His voice was expressionless. "Seen what I have seen, Mistress. We questioned the station while still in space, and it confirmed that it had no record of welcoming Linh aboard."

Quyen thought of the Honoured Ancestress' serene voice, telling her that She could lie. That She had lied, and that the false records were already on their way to the Embroidered Guard. And she knew that it was not a malfunction, but, rather, that the Honoured Ancestress had had to choose between failing its duty of protection or failing its programmed rules. And She had made a decision, in the end. Gone against all that was expected of her.

Like Linh.

"The station itself seems to have no record of anything past fifty years ago. I can only presume you've suffered some severe malfunction in the meantime. My sympathies." The Embroidered Guard's mouth turned inwards at the corner. "But I see no reason to disbelieve any of this."

"I need…" She swallowed, aware of her presumption. "If I might have a word with her, before she leaves?" She kept her eyes on the floor, saw it become stained, as if with rust; saw the patches of iridescent colours playing across her skin.

Soon. Soon she would feel the familiar presence, the warmth in her chest. She would no longer feel hollow, emptied of everything.

But it was a lie, and she knew it.

The man made a gesture Quyen couldn't see. "Fine. You have five minutes." He stepped away in a swish of silk robes.

Quyen rose, found herself facing Linh across an array of Embroidered Guards who showed no sign of moving. What were they afraid of? That she'd try to run? As if she would. Linh's face was paler than usual, but perfectly composed. Something had returned to her, a lethal grace akin to Lady Oanh's, a set cast to her features that gave her the air of a statue in a temple. A magistrate's face, that of the law, and nothing else.

"I have your package," Quyen said.

Linh's lips stretched. It might have been meant as a smile, but it was the most frightening expression Quyen had seen, utterly devoid of anything but a savage joy. "I'm glad, Cousin."

"You made your intent more than clear, yet again. Was there no more subtle poetry you could have found?"

Linh shrugged. "Perhaps. It doesn't matter." She spread her hands. "Was there anything else, Cousin?"

It matters, demons take you. It matters because I need to understand why you did this, why you did any of this. Quyen found her hands were shaking. With an effort, she stilled their trembling.

"Please," she said, and found herself blinking furiously to clear the tears in her eyes. "I need to—"

"—to control everything, as you've always done." Linh's voice was flat, but not angry. "To rule the only thing you can rule in your life."

Her husband Anh, lost in the turmoil of war. The Honoured Ancestress, beyond her grasp now, her memories gone into the darkness. Xuan Rua, who might never forgive her for Huu Hieu's suicide attempt. "No," Quyen said. "You don't understand."

Linh smiled. And, for the first time, the expression was almost girlish, carefree. "Oh, I do understand. Far too much, Cousin. Some things make sense because they fit into the harmony of the world."

"Moral principles?" Quyen all but spat, not sure why she wanted to take Linh and shake some sense into the girl. "And you find them now?"

"Perhaps." Linh's gaze moved away, towards the tube-door and the ship, and the capital, and the trial that awaited her. The trial that had but one possible outcome.

"For what is worth, because we share blood, though neither of us acted as if we did. Because we are family, and a family might quarrel, but should never tear itself apart. I wish you well, Cousin Quyen. You and everyone aboard Prosper. May you all see ten thousand years of peace." She turned away, started walking towards the waiting ship, the Embroidered Guards moving with her like a tide.

"Cousin!" Quyen called, as Linh was almost gone. "All the same. Thank you." The words were like acid against her tongue, like the mem-implants, things she couldn't hold for long without feeling burnt. "You'll be welcome among us, should you choose to come back."

Linh didn't answer, but Quyen thought she saw her nod. At the last moment, before she vanished within the ship, she turned and nodded to Quyen, from equal to equal. And in her eyes, Quyen saw everything: the pain, the grief, barely held at bay; the fierce anger, and the resolution to be more than that anger, to be more than a failed magistrate, to die for her cause…All of it, flung into Quyen's mind like the cold of deep spaces, until she found herself shaking, tears running down her face.

"I'm sorry," she said, but Linh had moved, and could no longer hear her. "I'm sorry."

Quyen stood in the rising silence, watching the light pool on the walls beside her. She waited for the moment when the Honoured Ancestress would awake; when she,

Quyen, would walk away from the docks, the Honoured Ancestress in her mind, and guide Prosper and its family into the future with her, as she had always done.

She waited for the moment when she would no longer be alone.

They let Linh remain in the aft bay of the Mind-ship. After all, with all the doors closed, where else could she go but into the emptiness of space? She stood, watching Prosper slowly recede behind them. The lights, strangely enough, seemed to shine brighter and brighter with every moment, as if the station itself still sought to reach out to her.

A sick mind's fancy, no doubt. Prosper's Honoured Ancestress had never cared much for her, and was no doubt glad to be rid of an unwelcomed visitor.

The commander of the Embroidered Guard had told her, stiffly—as if he couldn't quite resign himself to the necessity of communicating with a criminal—that there had already been pleas in the capital. That she wouldn't find herself without allies there.

She thought of Lady Oanh, of the vast resources at the other's disposal. Perhaps she could indeed avoid it, all of it, and its fated ending.

Or perhaps she couldn't. But her memorial remained and its words, perhaps, in time, would be heeded. Perhaps the Empire would once more be united, just as families that fell out could, in the end, be reconciled to each other.

"That was a noble thing you did," the commander

had said. Puzzled, as if he couldn't quite understand why she'd refused to drag the station down with her. As if people did that, all the time. But of course, she thought, we're small-minded and petty, and sometimes, we let ourselves be hollowed out by hatred. And sometimes, we commit the unforgivable.

She watched the station recede away from her, its lights slowly blinking. No, she thought, chilled, it was no illusion. The lights *were* growing more intense, almost blinding. Not all of them, but the single one in the docking bay, where Quyen would still be standing.

As she watched, it winked, slowly, and shifted to a warm red, the colour of banquet halls, of luck. It held the hue for a full eight heartbeats, before shifting back to the deep yellow of the Emperor and the Imperial Court—her cousin's wishes for good fortune that Linh would carry with her like a lifeline, all the way into the heart of the divided Empire.

Read on for a Sneak Peek of
The Latest Xuya Universe Novella

In the Shadow of the Ship

Forthcoming Fall 2024

KHUYÊN HADN'T EXPECTED to ever come back to her birthplace.

She'd run away from *The Nightjar, Thirsting for Water* when she was sixteen. She'd left behind the ruined mindship and her endless travel between the stars, her desperate hurtling away into the vast darkness of space, her steadfast quest for a refuge that the Numbered Planets—ravaged from decades of war—couldn't provide. Khuyên had left behind, too, her family and their unshakeable devotion to the ship's demands and needs.

And now, here she was.

Because Grandmother was dead, and Khuyên's colleagues—like her, all officials in the service of the Dragon Throne—had spoken of duty. Of the value of honouring one's ancestors. Of the necessary period of mourning. And because—on some level—Khuyên still felt guilty for running away—for failing to do her duty to uphold the order of the world, for abandoning her family.

Khuyên had taken an imperial mindship to the periphery, and from there a shuttle to the isolated planet where *Nightjar* was due to dock. And when *Nightjar* had arrived—when she had loomed out of the darkness of space, shimmering like some monster out of myth, the rusted paint on her pitted and cratered hull glittering as white as funeral clothes, as white as sorrow—Khuyên had fought the spike of fear that sent her heartbeat faster and faster at the thought of facing those she'd left behind.

She'd reminded herself, again and again, that she was a magistrate of the Đại Quang district on the Sixty-Fourth Planet, and her duties lay elsewhere. That she'd made a choice to leave all of it behind—family, ship, and everything else—and that she'd felt few regrets over the past four years.

It had helped, but not that much.

Now Khuyên was in the old reception room with her bots clustered around her, feeling naked and vulnerable—as if everyone could see her elevated heartbeat, the sweat on her skin—the roiling mass of fear and guilt within her that threatened to burst out.

"You haven't touched your tea," Mother said.

Khuyên sipped it. It was served in celadon that looked too smooth and new—and the tea itself tasted of sharp grass. She felt the rough surface of the cup beneath her fingers: *Nightjar* had been badly damaged in the war and had only fragmentary overlays, most of her non-critical processing powers being reserved for animating avatars and appearance overlays. Unlike most mindships Khuyên had seen as an adult, *Nightjar* didn't project an avatar, human or otherwise, to mingle with people. In fact, she couldn't speak to anyone except in her heartroom, where so few had been trusted to enter.

So there was nothing to feel or see in Khuyên's hands

but the cup itself—no sweeping ornamentations, no vivid imprint of animals moving across the surface, no smell or sound of water or of the stars. The cup felt stark and bare and devoid of artifice, and the reception room likewise was the inside of a ship's cabin: a table of polished steel and two utilitarian chairs, a metal floor and metal walls with only a few physical pictures.

Nevertheless, Khuyên could still feel *Nightjar* around her; the weight of the ship's presence; the soft patter of her bots in the vents and in the walls; the multiple sensors she had watching them, two people in a single room on a single floor, among the thousands of people scattered on *Nightjar's* long and cavernous eighteen floors. She was watching them even with all the privacy locks Khuyên had raised before she went onboard—and Heaven only knew what she made of all of this. Of any of this.

"How have you been?" she asked, bracing herself for a nebulous blow.

Mother looked unchanged: her hair a little grayer, her lean face a little more hollowed-out, but she still carried herself with the same poise, the same elegance: her top-knot flawless, the gold ornaments glittering in the dim light; wearing a soft pink five-panel dress as if it were imperial garb. In overlay, the peaches on Mother's dress glittered and went from flower to seed to stone, to fully ripe fruit. "We've made do." Her gaze was sharp: she held Khuyên's until she had to look down, obscurely ashamed. Mother's bots—two things small enough to fit on the back of her hand, half-broken sensors glittering in the dim light—wrapped around her wrist, their multiple, spider-like legs gripping the peach silk cloth. "I hear you've been making your way in the world."

Khuyên gripped the cup. "Really? I thought news of outside didn't reach you." It wasn't quite true: news did filter in, fragments of newscasts and official Empire vids, picked up as the ship neared planets to refuel. Some people ignored them; some people gloried in the devastation outside, and in the knowledge they were safe.

"Sometimes," Mother said. "Just as news of the funeral reached you." She sipped her own tea. "You were always such a bright child." She sounded grudgingly proud.

The praise was unexpected, like water given to the thirsty or knowledge to the ignorant. Mother had given so little of it when Khuyên was a child: sometimes it felt like Khuyên couldn't move or breathe without drawing criticism.

"Of course, you were less interested in anything to do with social. Tell me, do you have a partner?"

Khuyên looked up, startled. "I—"

"Ah, never mind. Of course not. And no descendants. I should have known." Mother set the cup down. "Well, no matter. The funeral is tomorrow, and I have many things to prepare for. Good night, child."

Khuyên's voice seemed to have dried up. She said, finally, "Tell me." It felt unsteady and weak, not at all like that of a magistrate.

Mother paused in the doorway, one hand lingering on the metal frame. "Yes?"

"The Tribute."

Mother turned, watched her. Weighed her.

"Is it still going on?"

A silence. "Why? Are you going to denounce us? To bring the might of the Empire down upon us?"

The thought sent chills of panic into Khuyên's chest—that *Nightjar* would be arrested, her family taken away to jail or the lacerators, all because of what she'd said— "No! Of course not."

"So you haven't *totally* strayed from what is right. Good."

"That's not—" Khuyên found her hands shaking. She thought of the missing children. The ones taken. She thought of Bảo—eight years old and always running lopsided, always singing at the top of his voice no matter how out of tune he was. Of Phi Phi and the way she'd always chew on her bots when trying to work out a particular problem, and the way they'd helped each other with their topknots as twelve-year-olds. Of the way, one day, they just hadn't been there anymore. "That's not what I'm asking."

"You were always better with written words," Mother said. And, more softly, "You know the Empire you serve has no sway here. Never has had. It has broken into ten thousand pieces, and I suppose the best it can send is you."

"I'm here for a funeral," Khuyên said, firmly, except that she felt sixteen again, as if she'd been caught stealing money. "Grandmother's funeral. And then I'll leave."

Mother watched her, unmoving. "Of course," she said. "Paying your respects. Good," Mother said, and left, without turning back—and Khuyên dug her fingers into the palms of her hands, because she wanted so badly to call Mother back.

Acknowledgments

This was first published more than a decade ago. Since then, the universe it's part of—the Universe of Xuya—has grown to include more novellas, two novels and a series of short stories that has allowed me to meld Vietnamese culture and space opera. It has allowed me to put in a science fictional setting the stories I grew up with—the stories of my family, the stories of war and diaspora, and of enduring in faraway times and places. My deepest thanks to everyone who has read this story and all the others, and to everyone who passed on the word.

I would like to thank, for the original edition, the Written in Blood writers' group (Dario Ciriello, Traci Morganfield, Genevieve Williams, Doug Sharp, Janice Hardy, Keyan Bowes, Juliette Wade), the awesome Rochita Loenen-Ruiz for steadfastly supporting me as a writer, and Carmelo Rafala for publishing it.

For this edition, I would like to additionally acknowledge: Tara O'Shea for backcover design, John Berlyne at Zeno Literary Agency, Joshua Bilmes, Lisa Rodgers, and Christy Admiraal at JABberwocky for making it possible.

And finally, to my friends both close by and faraway: thank you for being there.

About the Author

Aliette de Bodard lives and works in Paris. She has won three Nebula Awards, an Ignyte Award, a Locus Award, a British Fantasy Award and six British Science Fiction Association Awards.

She is the author of the lesbian space pirates romance *The Red Scholar's Wake*, a standalone book set in the same universe as this one, and *Of Charms, Ghosts and Grievances* (JABberwocky Literary Agency, Inc, 2022 BSFA Award winner), a fantasy of manners and murders set in an alternate 19th Century Vietnamese court.

She's also the author of *Navigational Entanglements* (Tor.com, 2024), a xianxia-inspired sapphic space opera, where four bickering juniors from navigator clans must learn to work together to hunt down a deadly creature from the void of space.

Visit her website http://www.aliettedebodard.com for free fiction (including further short stories set in the same universe as this one), Vietnamese and French recipes and more.